TO: FRANK

MR. C

THE AUTHOR

STILL PLAYA

CLIFTON HICKEY

STILL PLAYA

iUniverse books may be ordered through booksellers or by contacting:

iUniverse
1663 Liberty Drive
Bloomington, IN 47403
www.iuniverse.com
1-800-Authors (1-800-288-4677)

ISBN: 978-1-5320-1819-0 (sc)
ISBN: 978-1-5320-1820-6 (e)

Library of Congress Control Number: 2017902844

Print information available on the last page.

iUniverse rev. date: 04/20/2017

PROLOGUE

"STILL PLAYA'"

IT WAS ALL A DREAM...or so it seem. The perfect marriage. Wonderful kids. A peaceful life. Before it all, Nard couldn't BEGIN to imagine just how enjoyable tying the knot could really be. At least, that is, until the green grass on his side of the fence went unmowed or run-ins with the law became a normal trend. What lies ahead, only time and prayer can keep their vows bonded over troubled waters.

CHAPTER 1

He peered out over the still terrain in deep thought for being here in the first place. Headstones in perfect columns and rows surrounded by freshly lawn grass. It was mid-spring and his early dawn visit usually allowed him private time which he cherished every second of. He released a long sigh before lowering himself to the ground.

"Honey, I'm home," his face laced with a grin. "How you feeling on this wonderful Saturday morning young lady. Me, I'm so-so. Steady learning more about the true meaning of life and let me tell you, it'll take two lifetimes to figure this crazy world out. So much has changed over the last few years Grandma. Some good but for the most part, not so good. Much more betrayal now and the lies, Grandma, I had a lady that was looking me straight in the eyes and tried telling me three lies in three seconds. UNBELIEVABLE! The world is burning now faster than it ever has but somehow, I still manage to maintain my sanity. Must be genetics and by the way, allow me this wonderful opportunity to thank you for allowing me to be a part of the Jarrett's heritage. Our family are strong people by nature. Just like those two great-grandkids of yours grandma who are both doing fine. Asia, or shall I say miss angel-face, is growing tall as a tree. You know Grandma, I think I never told you why she was given that nickname which is because when she was a baby and would be asleep, I would walk in the room calling her name and she would always awake instantly with a smile on her face. Very similar to the one you used to embrace the family with. As for your great-grandson, for some reason he gets the impression that he's the man of the house and I have no problem with that. Only when he feels like he's big enough to involve himself with drugs or alcohol is when big-poppa steps up to the plate and intervene. You know, slow him down a lil'. As for your daughter she's doing just fine. I think I'll pay her a visit later on today to make sure she's keeping the peace. Well Grandma', I think this is the moment where we say our prayers together. Would you mind having the honor in saying it for us today? Thank you," lowering his head in silence. The emotional moment forced a tear drop down side of his face. "Amen," wiping away its stain. He replaced the shrivel rose in its vase at the head of her tombstone with a yellow one and rose to his feet. "I love you grandma' and always, ALWAYS continue saying your prayers for the family. I guess I'll be headin' back into the world we call hell now. As always, I enjoyed your company. Take care grandma," walking off.

THREE YEARS EARLIER.....

CHAPTER 2

"Sooooo which one of you young ladies could find yourselves spending the rest of your life with me?"

"After the way you just finished workin' me down in between," commented Kanisha, "I would've thought you already had proposed to me."

She quickly smothered his lips with hers before being shoved to his side.

"GIRL," intervened Kandi positioning her entire nakedness atop of his, "I'm ready to fight for mines at any time on the drop of a dime."

Her tongue caressed his chin all the way underneath its arch and down side of his neck.

"Well, I guess we'll just have to share him. Move yo' butt over some."

M-J knew of the twins all too familiar from high school on the cheerleader team. Their dark skin tone had its way of attracting over half the football team during practice. Him and several of his friends usually huddled together before drills viewing them off from a distance while fantasizing about how enjoyable a night would be with either of them. He caught sight of the trouble they were experiencing in the parking lot after practice and decided to lend a helping hand.

"Mind if I be of some assistance?"

"You could try and see what it is causing this damn car to not start," mentioned Kandi somewhat agitated.

"Is the gas hand on E?"

"Very close," answered Kanisha.

"Is the fuel injection light on?"

She eyed through the partial leather and woodgrain steering wheel. "Yeah"

"Well, that's clearly out my league. Your car will have to be towed in for reservicing from wherever you purchased that girlie' look'n' plastic from."

Kandi stated, "Ain't nuthen' plastic bout' this Lexus baby. More than I can say for that drug dealer lookin' car you driven' around in with those big ol' rims you got on it. I might can't even get myself up in the seat that thing sits so high up."

"Will you quit trippin' so much, Kandi, and let's just get in."

He remained quiet for most of the ride while they went back and forth in conflict.

Finally deciding to disrupt their dialogue, "Both of y'all are like night and day I suppose?"

"It's called balance. Kandi the enforcer and me, the peace maker."

"That's understanding. But since I have you two in the presence of this donk and that I also don't mean to sound too inquisitive, but being this y'all last year of school, what's next?"

"Love, life and just plain ol' living," replied Kandi.

"Just that simple."

"Don't believe that fool M-J. Kandi is going off to UGA and I'm going to Spellman."

"And still, love, life and living. Just like I said, M-J, you're only a sophomore on the honor roll and the star running back which is a good thing. So most likely, you'll end up with a scholarship to attend a great college as well."

"You're intelligent. Witty. Sexy too but you didn't hear it from me," smiled Kanisha.

"The same thing me and the rest of the boys think about you two beautiful ladies back at school."

"Thank you M-J," replying together.

"Being that y'all are so identical, does that make the competition amongst you two that much stronger? I mean, intense? As in, who can do this or that the best? Like, which one of y'all cooking the best?"

"That would be me, okay," retorted Kandi.

"Not hardly girl."

"Well, how bout' who's the fastest or who does the best split?"

"We fare somewhat the same in track and field as well as cheerleading," answered Kanisha.

"What about love making," josh M-J.

"What about who," spoke Kandi slightly confused at the question.

"You know, who puts it down the best?"

"Now how in the world we suppose to know that when we be with two different men behind two different closed doors at two different times," asked Kanisha.

"Don't try and act like the thought never crossed y'all minds before at least once. I mean, me personally, I think the experience could do more good than harm. Especially after witnessing each other in rhythm. If you ask me, the competition couldn't do nothing but improve y'all sex life."

"Boy, you are a fool," mentioned Kandi.

"But not a fool for being curious," implied Mike. Kanisha glanced around at her sister who stared back in return. "Anyway, look here ladies, I got to run inside real quick to grab something. Be right back."

He pulled in front of his driveway and walked up to the house.

"YOU JUST GONNA' LEAVE US OUT HERE LIKE THAT," yelled Kandi.

"YEAH! YOU COULD'VE AT LEAST INVITED US IN FOR A SECOND OR TWO," added Kansisha.

The expression written across their faces informed him of regretting it for the rest of his life if their request wasn't granted.

"Be careful steppin' out the donk! It's a long fall down!"

The thrilling thought of having experienced a sexual encounter with twins was hidden underneath his face the whole time they lay together. To hear them in conflict of wanting to share him meant satisfaction at the highest degree. He knew his friends wouldn't have believed him through word-of-mouth which is why he recorded the entire episode from a hidden camera installed in one of his trophies located on the bedroom dresser.

"Did I hear a door just slam," Kanisha uttered inching her head upward off his arm.

"Shawty', you trippen'! That's just yo' mind reawakening itself inside your head."

"I'm serious M-J. I know I heard someone outside that door."

Busting into his room, "MIIIIIIIIIIIIIIIIIIIIIIIIIIIIIIIIKKE JUUUUUUUUNIIIIOUUUUUUUUUUUUURR!"

CHAPTER 3

"**B**OOOOOY! That damn child of yours! I'm gone kill'em"

"What he do now," asked Mike.

"Mike! I'm gone kill his ass!"

"What he do?"

"How soon can you get yo' butt to the crib?"

"I'm in traffic right now. It'll be like, ten minutes or so."

"You betta' try makin' it in one cause he only got less than that before I start choken him out."

The last time he remembered her this enraged was when their son set aflame her favorite love seat at the age of eight. Judging by her actions today, the incident seemed worse. He just hoped she wouldn't flip out and go on some type of rampage before he got there. Mike preferred talking it out first and finding a solution later. A method Shenequa considered a waste of time. Several vines twisted together or a belt suited her fine. She stood outside their home up against the car. In tears.

"Damn baby! You aiight'?

"Mike…why me," wiping her face. "I've done everything possible to try and make our child happy and this is how he repays me?'

"What he do?"

"He-he! I can't even get it out. Go talk to him. He's in there," pointing at their home.

"You gonna' be aiight' out here?"

"Hurry up and go save his ass cause it aint' too late for me to kill him."

8

Whatever the problem was, Mike knew she was just seconds away from causing serious bodily harm to their only child. He knocked on the bedroom door.

"Who that?"

"Who that! It's yo' dad. That's who. You mind if I come in?" Mike had already entered before his son could answer him. "Yo' mother wants you dead which could only mean you've effed'-up pretty damn good."

"Yeah dad. That, I've done."

"Now me and you have been able to talk about anything no matter how right or wrong you were and that still remains to this day. But I must ask you this as I always have in the past...why? Why? WHY?"

"Tryin' to be cool dad."

"Tryin' to be cool. That's a start but you mean cool as in tryin' to impress someone-like cool.

"Sort of."

"Tryin' to make someone happy?"

"In a way."

"Tryin' to please someone?"

"Two to be exact."

Mike pondered on his son's last answer before finally figuring it out.

"And you couldn't have found no other place beside bringing them here?"

"Everything happened so fast dad! Before I knew it, they were both asking to come inside which we ended up in my bedroom where momma later burst open the door. What was I to do dad? Tell them, 'No ladies. My parents are not home. Therefore, I can't have any company'."

"We didn't have a problem with you inviting them into the living room but into your bedroom and on your bed. BOTH of them? One should've been yo' lookout or something."

"That would have been the smartest thing to do. But not only was it two of them dad but they were twins."

"TWINS! Get out of here!"

"I'm serious dad."

"Damn! That's one way for a young man to step his game up."

'MIKE," barging in, "I know got-damn well I just didn't hear you say anything to our son about him stepping his game up?"

"Nah baby."

"Negro, don't lie to me."

"Shenequa, didn't you ask me to talk to him?"

"Yeah. But I'm taking over now. Mike Junior, you got before the sun goes down to pack yo' shit and get the hell out my house."

"Are you serious momma!"

"In fact, make it in one hour and by the time I come back from getting my mind right, you better be far gone."

"Can I at least explain a lil' of what happen?"

"BOY," stepping towards his direction.

"Do as your mother says son." He withheld her back and led her out the room. "You weren't really serious about putting him out were you?"

"Junior has to understand his position not only in life but definitely at home. He got plenty friends. He'll be aiight'. If not, there's plenty of room underneath the Chattahoochee River Bridge."

"You're cold. Did you know that?"

"You wanna' join him? Well, keep taken' this so lightly and you'll be next." She stepped into their bedroom slamming the door in his face.

CHAPTER 4

"**Y**ou wouldn't believe what happened at the house yesterday."

"Without caring, I suppose you gone tell me anyway."

"Tosha, you know what you pass due for…an ass whoopen'. Starting at the chest first. Swell up those baby C-cups some which will probably help you find a man somewhere out there in the world."

"I already got that at your house except for when you're away, he tells me how good the kitty-kat taste."

"It's yo' mouth that I find the most amazing thing about you cause that what comes out of it finds much relief in not having to go back into those penis-puckers of yours."

"MISS penis-puckers to you hata'."

"Let me finish tellen' you what happened cause I'm on my way to an important business meeting. Would you believe that my son, Michael Turner Junior, would consider our house to be one of his play-pen as well as doing what-so-ever he chooses to do in his bedroom?"

"I thought you said you had somewhere important to be?"

"Why, is there a problem?"

"Yes! You taken' too damn long to say what it is. My cornes on my feet are killin' me and I would like to get back to soaking them in some Epson salt. An ol' school family tradition shared by my mother."

"I caught him. In bed. With two naked girls. Twins at that! Aint that something? I wanted to kill the poor child on sight.

"Mm, mm, mm. Sounds like to me he's a product of his mother."

"Woman, you sound like a damn fool."

"Wasn't that you in the high school bathroom with a line as long as the welfare line allowing boys to view more that the tattoo between yo' legs?"

"You know what, you damn right and when it was all over, I allowed you to come and clean me off... with your tongue!"

"And where is this Mr. Mike Steele at now?"

"Out my house and living on his own."

"You didn't?"

"You need a place to stay? I got a vacant room for you and all you have to do is takeover one house bill. Any more questions?"

"I guess that's a good way of learning from your mistake by cutting him loose at the umbilical chord. Finding a way to really be grown and eating on his own."

"He'll be aiight'. Just don't let him trick you into staying with you for a while."

"Why not? Shoot, the boy IS fine with muscles. He can do me and my lonely world much good."

"You heard what I said. NO! HELP!"

"I got you child."

"Let me get out of here."

"And please don't come back no more today unless you're bringing M-J to my rescue."

She showed Shenequa the front door and reconvened on her toes.

CHAPTER 5

Nard hadn't to long left from picking his son up at school. He enjoyed their time alone while quizzing his son about class lessons or the homework his teacher might've assigned him.

"Hey, dad?"

"Yeah son."

"Can I ask you a question?"

"Talk to me."

"Why does my stepmother hates mommy so much?"

The question came as no surprise knowing the day would eventually come about the hostility brewing amongst his family but he hadn't figured today. His gaze lasted a brief moment in his son eyes contemplating on how to answer him.

"Jealously!"

"Jealously?"

"One wanting what the other don't have."

"And what is that daddy?"

"You sho' is nosy today. What y'all been talking about in class that got you asking so many questions?

"Nothing really. I was just wondering what my mommy done to Shontae. She says she has no problem with her."

"She doesn't."

"So what's wrong?"

"How bout' this, when you get a few more years of living under your belt, then we'll sit down and tell you everything you need to know. Daddy's promise?"

He extended a pinky out at his son who locked one in with him.

"Daddy's promise," sharing a grin.

"Now, how was your day?"

"It was good."

"Good as in great or good as in aiight'?"

"Aiight'."

"Could've been better?"

"Yeah. I guess. The teacher kept calling on me for most of the answers in class. All the other kids acted as if he wasn't even there. It's hard for me to hear him sometimes because of so much noise.

"The teacher allows all of that to happen during class?"

"He's a small fry. A nerdy looken' man. He talks like someone is squeezing his nose."

"How he sounds is not important but what is is you keepin' those grades up."

"Yes sir."

"I can't stress the importance of an education to you enough. Without it, you stand a great chance in living a miserable life. Remember this, a young boy carving his behavior into greatness is leaving no room for mistakes when he grows up. Now give yo' ol' man a hug before you get out the car."

"You not coming in the house to say hi to grandma'?"

"Not today. I got to get back home. Uncle Mike and M-J are on their way over to the house.

"Okay," reaching across the seat sharing hugs. "Bye daddy."

"I love you boy. And give grandma' a hug for me."

Nard watched his son trot towards the house. It hadn't really dawn on him just how fast he was growing up. Not long ago, he commented of never having any kids to his mother. Now, a wife and beautiful daughter at home and a son by a woman who continues to remain loyal as a friend. Shontae wasn't informed of his son until almost two years into their marriage. He believed any sooner notice would have possibly destroyed their togetherness and decided it was best if their love continued to grow stronger as time progress. Once informed, it took several months for her disdain to finally settle itself and accept the fact that it was a child, her husband child, vowing to support him the best way she knew how. She promised of any improper involvement with Peaches would send her and their daughter both packing only to never return. Nard kept most of his visits confidential. Peaches agreed to do the same out of respect for his marriage. Though her feelings for him never quite changed in over the past eight years, she somewhat admired his loving family and made no attempts at throwing herself on him. Strictly friendship.

CHAPTER 6

"**S**o tell us Uncle Nard, how should we deal with this young man who thinks he can do what he wants when he wants while living in the domain of someone else's home.?"

"Well sir, I say we thoroughly review the facts first before we do any pre-judging here in the courts today and then go from there. ALL RISE!" Mike and M-J stood up at the far end of the dining table while Nard stayed seated at the opposite end. "You both may be seated. The courtroom will now here the prosecutor version first. You may proceed with your opening argument Mr. Mike Senior."

"Thank you your honor. On August 20, which is yesterday, at or around six or six-thirty P.M. the defendant, Michael Turner Junior, took it upon himself to indulge in an act of coitus with not one young lady your honor but TWO within the vicinity of an area that he doesn't pay any house notes nor bills but only sleep, eat and shit in an area where everything is paid for."

"Is the individual with us in this here courtroom today Mr. Prosecutor?"

"Yes sir, your honor. He's seated right here to my left," pointing down at his son.

"Let it be noted for the record that the prosecutor has clearly identified the defendant in the courtroom today. You may proceed sir."

"Thank you your honor. The facts in this case today clearly outweighs themselves tremendously being that Mike Junior was caught in the act by the defendant's mother. And that, your honor, is my opening argument."

"Thank you sir. Alright, the defendant may state his opening argument as well."

"Uncle, y'all crazy."

"ORDER," pounding a cup down on the wooden table. "One more outburst like that in my courtroom sir and I'll hold you liable for disrupting the courts procedures."

M-J cleared the smile off his face pretending to take them serious.

"Aiight' unc', I mean, your honor. True enough, I was wrong. Very wrong! I'm not disputing that. But what about my teachings? My upbringing? If I'm not mistaken, it was you unlce that influenced me to socialize with a girl during y'all wedding reception when I was younger. And yes, I knew better than to allow myself to get caught up in an act that was totally ludicrous at my parents home. I'm not an adult yet but certain behavioral patterns were instill in me as a child to act in a certain way with girls while growing up and just so happen that way of lifestyle eventually caught up with me and two beautiful ladies at the wrong place and wrong time. Am I guilty? Of course I am! Am I wrong? Very! But am I fully to blame? NO! Sometimes, we all have to be careful what we wish for cause nine-times out of ten when it does come true, it is more than likely too much to accept and definitely too much to handle. That is all your honor. Thank you."

"Will the prosecutor please walk with me into a private location."

They went into his kitchen.

"Looks like we created a monster!"

"The boy got a strong case against you."

"I know. He came at us hard that time. Even alleged us in his act of wrong doing. Isn't that sort of like snitchen'?"

"You betta' say it is!"

"What you think I should do? I mean, ain't no doubt about it that he messed up but it looks as if we played our role in shaping his mind to."

"If it was me, I'll leave it up to wifey and hope, rather pray, that she's as nice as possible with him."

"Maybe she'll cool down eventually and accept him back in."

"Or maybe she'll deliver hamburgers and french fries to him at the shelter home. Only time will tell. Now lets try and bring this case to a close cause I got other things to do and so do you."

M-J looked on as they entered. Mike walked over next to him.

"Because the evidence in this case is suggesting some leniency doesn't mean that I'm not as mad as hell with you as your father is because I am but since I played a great role in tryen' to influence you as a child coming up to be a womanizer, I'm as much at fault as you are. So on those grounds, in the case of Mike Senior versus Mike Junior, I hereby find all three of us… GUILTY by association. This court is adjourne," pounding the cup down. "For future reference M-J, leave no room for mistakes because they can, and they will, come back to haunt you."

"Yes sir and dad," peering over at his father, "I'm sorry."

"I'm not the one you have to convince son. Though your mother would probably like a clearer understanding as in what was you thinking."

"I can't get her to even talk to me."

"She will. Just be patient.

"You know you facen' life behind bars don't you? Look at me when I'm talken' to you boy!" Trano lifted the man drooping head at the chin. "Four unregistered AK-47's. Two AR-15's. Four 9 Millimeter Beretta's. All with loaded clips! Son, what in the HELL was you thinkin'?

Trano studied the suspect demeanor weakened more as he slumped further down in his seat after mentioning an eternity behind bars. He recently graduated to commander-in-chief on the Alcohol, Tobacco and Firearms (ATF), after having served ten of his twenty years of law enforcement with the Federal Bureau of Investigation as an agent. The early half of his career involved two years as a police man and the rest with a local narcotics task force. He opted to involve himself at times with interrogations, homes and business raids which kept him away, for the most part, from excessive paperwork at his office desk. A part of the job he evaded at all cost. The suspect he held in custody was stopped by local police for speeding. Suspicious behavior led to a search of the vehicle recovering small amounts of marijuana hidden underneath the ashtray. A further search of the trunk revealed a large suitcase of artillery. They quickly alerted the ATF who took the suspect into custody downtown for questioning.

"Can I call my lawyer sir?"

"FO' WHAT! To tell him that his services are no longer needed! You're a convicted felon boy! We gone have a field day with this one. Oh yeah, me and the district attorney go waaaaay back in the day from rail-roading blacks to handing them large amounts of crack. You and your people just don't get it do you? This shit is bigger than King Kong and Godzilla both put together. You really want to know what C.I. A. stands for? Aiight' then, I'll tell you. It means Carrying-In-Airplanes shithead! That white stuff yo' community be killen' themselves with by selling it to each other, we got it by the tons. The government will do their part to make it look like they're tryen' to improve the poverish area but for the most part, WE, my crew and many other agencies, wouldn't be shit without those out there killen' their own kind. Now, when guns are involved, now we're probably talkin' about' people dyin'. Possibly my own and we know we can't be havin' that shit now can we?" He looked on with sadden eyes at Trano's face. "Good. So the only way to have a chance at savin' yo' black-ass is by what?"

"I-. I don't know man. How?"

"SNITCHEN' MOTHERFUCKER," pounding his fist on the small table, 'SNITCHEN'! Don't play dumb with me! You know how your kind do it. You ant' got to give up the whole world. Hell, you might accidentally give up some of my own people out there somewhere but I definitely want one. Someone who do a lot of rippin' and runnin' for you. Someone who got it quote-unqote 'Going on' as y'all would say in the hood." He tossed a Blackberry phone into his lap. "You still wanna' call your lawyer? By all means but let me say this, if you do, don't EVER in your fuckin' life look for some sort of plea deal with no federal, state or any local agency within a 2,200 hundred mile radius. Now, if you don't mind, I think I'll go sniff me a lil' stank-stank between my wife legs. You got one hour. Think smart. Do what you feel is best for you. Like I said, one funky ass hour, I'll be back."

CHAPTER 7

"**I**'ve been in business now for how long Trish?"

"Four years, eight months and two and a half weeks to be exact. Thank you very much," grinned Trish.

"You should know! As much as you hang around inside and outside her business," professed Shannon. "Do you ever go to school child or do you find lingering amongst daily gossip more exciting to you?"

"I'm gettin' my education but I'm also gaining plenty of business sense as well. Along with socializing skills of course cause if I can put up with you ladies pickin at me half the day, the rest of the world should be a piece of cake."

"Which is exactly why I allow you to work in my shop after school. You've shown great responsibility as well as keepin your grades up. Not many kids of our race has the type of advantages that you do young lady."

"You are so right," concurred Ms. Jones. "What you're doing by allowing her the opportunity to better herself is something all of us black business owners should be partaking in which is lettin' the youth get some type of feel or evolvement in the corporate world. A real taste at what it means to be productive in this society of ours today instead of our young sisters just wearing thongs up the butt in magazines or videos. Ain't nothing wrong with dreaming big but when your dreams exceeds your reality by another world, then its time to come back to 100th and 10th Street and focus on what's important today so your tomorrow has a stronger chance in establishing yourself a greater opportunity for success."

"Preach Ms. Jones," applauded Shannon.

Peaches friendship with Ms. Jones progressed as a student of her cosmetology program which ended up being her long-term mentor. Since the grand opening of Lady's Luck Hair Salon several years ago, Ms. Jones occasionally stops by in admiration of her business and a minor touch-up as well. A little less than a third of the sixty thousand dollars she saved up in the bank before D-Man's death was used to finance her new-found establishment. Trish resided a block away having to walk pass the place going and coming from school every day. She offered free services around the shop with small chores due to her strong passion as a child with wanting to do hair. Peaches accepted her generosity and in return taught her the basic fundamentals of a hairstylist. She soon allowed Trish to practice what she learnt but only on school friends.

"I think that our race leans towards ignorance, for the most part, because of our laziness. The Caucasians run this world with an iron fist. Hell, why can't we? Sister's, it's time we start being each other cheerleaders. Show a lot more motivation towards being someone of significance cause if not, we're soon to be doomed as a race."

"That sounds good and everything Ms. Jones but what about all the hate and negativity that's spewing out all over the news and television towards each other," mentioned Shannon. "Just look at all the reality shows. Every third word that comes out they mouth is either a b this or b that. That sort of exposure to our youth can and will cause them to behave in the same manner. So you tell me, what are we to do in this devilish world of ours?"

"Well sistas', the only thing that I can say about it is … WE ARE FAAMILY," clapping her hands, "I GOT ALL MY SISTAS' WITH ME! Come on yall! Sing it with me!"

"WE ARE FAAAAMILY" the entire salon joing in, "I GOT ALL MY SISTERS WITH ME!"

"ONE MORE TIME NOW," shouted Peaches.

"WE ARE FAAAAMILY … EVERYBODY GET UP AND DANCE!"

The entire room danced around in joy knowing that a better tomorrow is destine to come.

CHAPTER 8

"You mind sharing with me how your day went or should I share my hectic venture with you first?"

"My boss can be very obnoxious at times. Even when you're performing at your best. Don't you know this man had the nerves to tell me about how my dress was exposing to much cleavage or how it's too tight at times."

"Maybe he's right."

"You taking sides with him?"

"You are at a job sight where you must perform in a professional manner. Sound to me like he might be expecting a more conservative appearance out of you. Or maybe he wants none of the boys looken' at you. You ever thought about that?"

"I have caught him ogling over me from in his office at times. Maybe I should've checked his butt then."

"How will you go about handling it now?"

"First thing tomorrow, I'll catch him in his office, small talk a lil' first then …BAM! 'Do I look like your wife or something! So why are you sheltering me so much!'"

"That sounds like a plan to me."

Shontae hadn't mention to her husband just how appealing her boss is. He was a few years younger. Single. Wealthy. She's been invited with him on a couple of business meetings in the past which turned out to be more of a social gathering. Temptation never crossed her mind about him but occasionally, he would mention of how beautiful she was at thirty-four and embraced his compliment with much gratitude.

"Kedar wanted to know earlier today why you and his mother are always beefin with each other."

"And what did you tell him?"

"Nuthen' but wait til' he's older and then we'll concern ourselves with that."

"I don't really hate her you know."

"Hanging up in her face. Not allowed to come by here without your permission first. Never sharing 'hello's' when the two of you pass each other in traffic and the list goes on."

"Well, maybe a lil' distaste."

"She'll be aiight'. Just don't allow your precious heart to harden itself due to ya'll differences experienced in the past. Can you promise you'll do that for me?"

"Only if she stays out my way. I won't make no sudden move."

"Aiight' Miss Gangsta'," smiling together. "Now that I've saved the best topic for last, you wouldn't believe who done what yesterday. In fact, we even had to hold court here at the house earlier today."

"What are you talken' about Nard?"

"M-J"

"What about him?"

"The boy was caught in the act at home with not one but TWO girls. TWINS to be exact."

Raising up in bed, "ARE YOU SERIOUS?"

"Dead serious."

"By who?"

"Shenequa."

"Oooooh lawd! Where he at now? On a hospital bed? You know that woman don't discriminate on who she takes off on. Family definitely included."

"Believe me, she wanted to but insisted Mike resolve it temporarily until she settled down some. Then she finally came to her senses and kicked the boy out. So earlier today, we had a hearing about the scenario trying to find the root of his hideous act and you know what, me and Mike are to blame as much as M-J is for tryin' to make him a playa' at a very young age."

"And look what you did. Got that boy living in the streets. You'll have to make sure he's okay since you're partly to blame."

"You right," staring up at the ceiling. "Aaaah yes!"

"And what are you aaaahing about?

"Nuthen'. Just reminds me of the good ol' days."

"Me kicken' you out the house?"

"Nah' woman. Women eating out my hands and kissing at my feet. Such wonderful memories.

"And what about our memories?"

"What about them?"

"Don't I," resting her chin on his chest in bed, "create good times better than ever?"

"You do aiight' … for a married woman," teased Nard.

"Just remember one thing daddy," straddling her nakedness atop of his under the covers, "I always have the opportunity every night at making you say …."

Her hands clawed into his chest moving her hips around in a slow, slithery motion.

"DYNOMITE," yelled Nard.

"Need I say more?"

CHAPTER 9

It's been over a week and M-J's mother hadn't accepted any of his phone calls or responded to any other attempts he made with contacting her. She even threatened to inform the law of trespassing if he stepped one foot on her lawn. He slept the first couple of nights in his car in the parking lot of a truck stop a couple of miles out of town. To ashame to inform anyone of his abandonment. Food consisted mainly of ramen noodle soup. He bathed in a pond he used to fish at that was swamped by trees and numerous signs of "'NO TRESSPASSING'" posted all around. Johny Blocka' noticed his weariness at school and enquired of the matter. Without delayence, he permitted M-J to reside at his family home for as long as he needed. He appreciated the offer finding refuge in their cluttered basement. M-J's father kept him updated on his mother's anger that continued to remain unchanged. A clear sign she had the slightest intention of changing her mind anytime soon.

"Hurry up and plug that thing up Blocka'. This what I got to show you here, you probably won't believe it."

"Probably not even after I witness it with my bare eyes either. How do I know this disc you got is the real thing? For all I know, this might be some bootleg shit you got here. You know this new millennium internet thing has images of people that's not even that actual person. R-Kelly! Perfect example.

"Homeboy, haven't I done nuthin' but kept it real with you since day one?"

"One-thousand to be exact."

"So what reason do I have now to change up the game on you?"

"None I hope."

"Hoping is for the hopeless so save it. But everything you're about to witness hasn't been exposed to no one but you until I decided what I'm gonna do with it."

"Don't tell me you plan to sell copies of it?"

"And why not."

"Look man, them girls got dreams dawg' and this won't do nuthin' but cramp their style."

"That's not my actual plan but who knows. It might make them movie stars. The coin toss can go both 50-50. Lets just expect the best."

Johny Blocka' watched the devilish expression take form on M-J's face and started up the DVD with its remote.

"AAAAH-MAN! Are you serious! Look at their body's! Damn those girls fine as hell! BOY," glancing at M-J, "I GOT to give you yo' props for this one cause if what I'm lookin' at is the real-deal, then you ARE the real-deal playa'-pimp."

"What can I say bra.' All in a days work."

"And well worth the stay on my couch too! I wouldn't trip neither if I got kicked out my house for something like this. Which one had the best sex or did they both feel the same?"

"Hard to tell big homie.' Though one va-ja-ja' was a bit tighter than the other which made the adventure that more thrilling."

"What's a va-ja-ja'?"

"A vagina my big, fury friend. Something that any civilized man can become crippled by and I'm not talking bout' being placed in a wheelchair either."

"We could run a vicious scheme with the boys at school by charging them to look at it," ejecting the disk.

"Hold up a minute big-fella'. First thing first. We have to make sure this doesn't fall into the wrong hands or there could be some helluva' consequences behind it and me being thrown out of school is one of them. Give me a minute to come up with something and I'll get back with you. And one more thing."

"What's that you big ol' pimp?"

"Please hit that light on you way out if you don't mind sir. A new day is almost amongst us and we need all the rest possible.

"Now you kicken' me out my own basement."

"Not really. Just being polite in saying," covering his face in the pillow, "good night!"

"I can respect that but only cause you've proved worthy. Is their any other request your heinous has before the servant departs?"

"Yes sir, there is. I like my eggs scrambled with a freshly squeezed orange juice for breakfast in the morning."

"Not a problem sir. But just remember to tell Alice in wonderland that I still got the hots' for her ever since I was six."

CHAPTER 10

"What you got in here to eat momma? I'm starven'."

"Nuthin' really. You need for me to scrounge you up something?"

"No momma. I'll get your grandson to preoccupy his un-busy time. BERNARD! BERNARD," yelled Ms. Hick from in her mother's kitchen.

"MAMM?"

"COME IN HERE BOY!"

"Why you bother that child? I told you I was gonna' put you something together."

"That's okay momma. You been feeding me for way to many years now and I sincerely thank you for it but now the cycle has changed and you have one of your many lovely grandchildren in the living room doing nothing but sitting on his rump. BERNARD!

"Yes mother. I'm right behind you."

"Not any mo' you ain't. Go over there and fix me and your grandmother something to eat."

"What would you ladies like?"

"Gone and have a seat son. I told your mother that I would cook something for her."

"Momma', it's to hot for you to be standing over some stove fryen' chicken. He knows what he's doing. I taught him very well back home."

"I already got some cornbread from yesterday wrapped up in the fridge. I'll put some greens on marinated in a ilil' vinegar and we'll go from there."

"Sounds like a plan to me momma. How bout' I give you a hand with that grandma'."

"You can start by cutten' up those greens in the refrigerator. You do know how to handle a knife don't you," teased grandmother. "So how is everyone back home?"

"Everything is fine grandma'. Chris and his family are all in one piece and Terry, well, he's just being Terry. Laying his hat down wherever he rest his feet at."

"And what about you son? How is everything back at the Ponderosa?"

"We good grandma'. Shontae and the kids send their hello's along with their blessings."

"Grandma' just glad we're all still breathing. Thank GOD for that. Now hand me that flour over their on the counter son."

"No problem grandma'."

He searched through several white containers before finding the right one.

"Momma'?"

"Yeah child."

"I been thinking. It's been almost four years since we gathered the entire family together at your place for a large cookout. A few of your kids out of town said they had no problem with it. The date was mainly all they're waiting on but I haven't talked to you yet."

"You know my house is always available for a good cause."

"So it's alright with you momma'?"

"Child, don't be acten' like you crazy with me. We've been gathering here at this house going on 50 years. You do all the family gathering you need and just let me know when the busses pull up outside my door."

"Say no more momma."

"That's just like my momma' grandma'. Always bossen' someone around as if she was put in charge of everything."

"I run you don't I?"

"To a certain extent."

"Only when you're a thousand miles away is when that extent is able to fully extend itself. Other than that, yo' butt is mine."

"If you say-so big-momma'."

"You two never quit do you," laughed grandma'. "What am I gonna' do with-"

She experienced a sharp pain in her chest unable to utter a word. Her body rested itself against the sink and placed a hand over the discomfort felt in her chest.

Ms. Hick and Nard rushed to her side.

"Momma' … what's wrong? You aiight'?"

"I … don't know. I feel … light headed."

"Come on grandma'. Let's have a seat."

They slowly walked her over to a chair at the table.

"Momma'. I'm callin' an ambulance."

"No child! I'll be," still feeling the pain, "alright."

"Call an ambulance son! Now! Hurry up!"

"I got you momma'!"

The ambulance didn't take but ten minutes to arrive and another ten to get her to the hospital. They waited inside the lobby for over thirty minutes for some type of news. Ms. Hick stood the entire time staring out a window at nothing in particular. Nard browsed through a complete stack of magazines repeating the cycle.

"Excuse me, Ms. –"

"That'll be me doctor," cutting short the doctors sentence.

"How you doing mamm," shaking her hand.

"How bad is it doc?"

"Honestly, not to good. She suffered a severe stoke and at her age, that can make matters very difficult. We're going to keep her here for a few other tests.

"Meaning?"

"Meaning, I can't give you a definite answer on how much longer she'll have to stay. A couple of weeks. Minimum."

"Doc', my mother hates hospital. Hell, even when she had me she wasn't present," shedding a little humor on the scenario. "You mind if me and my son go see her."

"You're really not allowed to at this time since we got her under strong dosage of medication but I'm sure a few minutes won't harm much. Walk straight ahead. Take a right. First door on your left."

"Come on momma'."

They sped down the hallway wasting no time. She lay motionless on a hospital cot unaware of their entrance.

"Momma'. Momma', it's me," brushing a hand along side her long streaks of gray hair.

"And your favorite grandson."

They weren't sure if she could hear them or not. Her heart rate appeared normal on the scanner. Tubes extending in an out her nose and arm. The sight made them both feel uncomfortable with the state of her condition.

"You gave us quite a scare back at the house momma'. A big one! I know how much you hate these places and as soon as we can we'll be getting' you out of here. The doctor said it shouldn't be but a few more days." A lie she hated to inform her of. She was always forward with her mother. Modest. Tears began to trickle down her face. "As soon as you're released momma', we're going to have that family cookout."

"And guess who's gonna' do some of the cookin' grandma'," holding on to her meaty hand, "ME! Along with a lot of your assistance of course."

"We would stay longer if we could but we were only permitted a few minutes. We don't suppose to be in here to be honest but the doctor was kind enough to let us see you." She planted a kiss across her forehead. "I love you momma'. Get well soon."

Seeing her mother laid out on a hospital bed for the first time scared her senseless. She never recalled her mother ever having to attend a hospital for any sort of illness. Miss Jarret stayed active **do**ing constructive deeds throughout her neighborhood or chores around the house which kept her in high spirits. How long she would have to stay replayed itself over and over in her mind the entire ride home. Nard hadn't spoken a single word, permitting his mother time to gather her private thoughts.

"Momma', she gone be okay. I know it."

"I hope you're right son. I'll definitely pray on it as soon as I step inside."

"Me to."

"Enjoy your evening son."

"I love you momma'."

"I love you to."

He waited until she made it inside safely before pulling off.

CHAPTER 11

Shontae waited outside his office door preparing her speech. Acting it out presented more of a task that she soon started having doubts about performing. Not once has it ever been a problem with addressing any work-related issues. His reaction to a personal matter is what worried her the most. He continued to rock back and forth with his back facing the door in laughs on the phone. She held a fist up to the window in hesitation. A long sigh finally placed her at ease before knocking several times. He swiftly spunt around with anger in his eyes. It didn't take long for the sign of displeasure structure across his face to settle back into a welcoming smile witnessing her standing outside his door. He waved her in. She took a couple of steps inside and refused to move any further.

"Mr. Smith. I need to-"

"Would you mind speaking up Mrs. Hick. I can hardly year you and please, call me Antonio."

Clearing her throat, "Mr. Smith, I mean, Antonio, there's something I need to say. Something I need to get off my chest."

"Well," taking a stand against the front of his desk, "what exactly is it you would like to talk to me about. Lets see … better work hours?"

"No sir."

"Alright. A raise?"

"Not really."

"I know what you want. A bonus!"

"Yes! No. Sir, Antonio, I'm getting the impression that you might feel as if I'm your personnel property. You know, your lady or something."

"Why Mrs. Hick, whatever gave you that impression," seeming perplexed.

"You informing me about excessive cleavage. Attire to tight. Sir, I've even caught you ogling at me."

"Mrs. Hick, If I misled you to believe such a thing, I truly do apologize but you and I both know that I like to keep my firm, our firm, in the tightest, most professional state at all times and just so happen, I view you to be an assistant at the top of the chain. Your demeanor needs to constantly establish an aura of natural respect not just around here but during board meetings and so on." He approached closer taking hold of her hand. She grew frighten unsure of his next move. "Shontae. You don't mind me calling you by your first name do you." Not a single word spoken. "Don't get me wrong, you are a beautiful person but it's your intelligence which exudes dominance about yourself. So do me a favor, take your talent and always inform yourself one thing," searching her eyes, "ones destiny is controlled by a thriving, more dedicated force. Please ... maintane it."

She felt relieved his hand had finally freed hers. He sat back down at his desk.

"I ... I think I'll be leaving sir, I mean Antonio."

"And anytime you feel the need to discuss a problem, my office is always open to you."

He picked up the phone reconvening what sounded like an earlier conversation. Her slow departure seemed forever exiting his office. She couldn't believe he had shifted the entire topic around to informing her about staying focus. Reclining in a chair at her cubicle gave her a sense of relief resting as far back as she could.

CHAPTER 12

"Is that a ghost just walked up in my shop?"

"Mm-hm'. Yep'. A handsome one at that," responded Shannon.

"How you ladies doing?"

"And what have I done to deserve an unannounced visit from you sir?"

"Not a thing Peaches. I'm just out and about payen' all my close friends and family visits. Making sure everyone is copacetic but since the day had exceeded over into the late evening, I thought I'd save the best visit for last."

"Flattery gets you babies around her so be careful how smooth you speak sir."

Waving his hands in surrender, "I wants noooo problem."

"But since you're here, there is something your service could be of some use for. My stereo in the back has a shortage in it or something cause the speakers keep fading in and out. Give me a minute to finish up her hair."

"You need to make it quick cause you know I gotta' move like a crook do when visiting you. Wifey wants our ties to only be because of our son needing something."

"This the millennium sir," intervene Shannon. "Don't your wife know that it's a blessing to be able to call you her husband with the female-to-male ratio being 8 to 1. She should be glad no one has tried to imprison yo' fine ass. No offense sir. But you need to tell her to be thankful there is a such law as marriage anymore cause it looks like in the years to come, a man will have the pleasure in having as many concubines he wants."

"Woman, pay-up so you can be-up out this chair and out my shop."

"Don't we sound desperate for some private time," digging in her purse. "Here! And you ain't keepin' no tip out of that so bring back all my chain. You blew that by bumpen' those wet-wet you speak between."

"Here's your chain. There's the door and please … don't look back."

"Pretty rough with them aren't you?"

"Only with those who got all the sense. Let me lock the front door right quick."

"But what about that problem Peaches?"

"Come with me. It's in the back." She led him down a short hallway. "There's the radio. Would you like something to drink?"

"Sure." He studied the Bose Stereo system noticing not a single wire behind it. "Peaches, you might have to send it back to the factory cause I can't see what might be the problem," grabbing hold of the ice cold Budweiser. "Good-lookin'."

"You say I might have to send it back?"

"More than likely. The latest technology made these days are all buttons and no wires. So how your business been holding up lately? Pretty good I suppose."

"She does what it do. Definitely keepin' the bills paid and our son clothed and fed."

"WE do those things."

"Bust mostly me."

"Mainly because you refuse majority of my help."

"You have your wife to blame for all that. She's the one who doesn't want you around here. So to keep the piece in your household, I only try and disturb you for something very important."

"That's very considerate of you. You're not a bad person after all."

"I never was. Just bad when I'm in bed."

"And good." He studied her smile admiring its genuine appeal. "Me and momms' had to rush my grandmother to the hospital today."

"Is the alright," questioning in serious concern.

"She's alive but the doc' said it's bad. A stroke was the cause of it all."

"I'm sorry to hear that Nard."

"Me and my grandmother are as tight as my mother. So this has me kind of shook up. Which is one of the main reason why I'm out payen' everyone visits. One day we're here and the next …it's like you never even existed. Damn I hope she pulls through."

"She will Nard. Lets keep our prayers strong."

She withheld him in a firm embrace.

"Peaches, it's getten' late. I'm sure wifey bout' wondering where I'm at."

"Oh yeah," releasing him, "I almost forgot."

"Forgot what?"

"You got to get back home to your perfect lil' family while this broken home make do."

He moved closer towards her on the couch.

"Don't say that Peaches. You still have a special place in my heart. You carried my first child. That shit means a lot to me."

"I sure as hell can't tell. Everything with us is only a 'hello' followed by a faster 'goodbye'."

"The girl don't want me know where near you."

"Is that what you want too? What does the ol' Nard have to say about that?"

"You wouldn't believe me if I told you."

"We got plenty of time. Our son is in great care with my mother. I'm listenin' as long as you speakin'."

He gulp the entire bottle.

"Let me have another one of these." She quickly obeyed his demand knowing he was in preparation of making himself comfortable. "Okay, to be honest with you," taking a long swallow, "I think about you sometimes, well a lot. One night, I accidently mumbled a portion of your name to her while maken' love. Fortunately, she was so busy into moaning and less in what I was sayin'."

"Why you dirty dawg'! Do you really miss me that much Nard?"

"Of course I do."

"Ahhhhh, that's so sweet," placing her lips on his cheek.

"But what I can't figure out is why your gorgeous self still single?"

"Because you're still married. Don't nobody interest my mind like you. I can listen to you talk all day and night. Your voice and words go together so perfectly. Those pretty lips. Handsome smile. I miss you Nard … and I mean that." Her hand brushed across the top of his head. "Your waves are pretty decent but I like the cornrows better."

"Me to but I had to elevate the appearance to a more professional presentation. I'm involved with more meetings now than selling cars so my swag has to emulate my status."

"Along with your professional sex game."

She smothered his mouth with hers. His body froze for a moment almost forgetting the true side of his life.

"Hold on a minute Peaches," pulling himself loose.

"Make love to me Nard. Right here! Right now!" Buttons at the top of her dress came unfasten. She slid it off her shoulders and stood up allowing it to drop entirely onto the floor. Nard stared in awe. Her bra removed next. "You can stop me when you get ready." He paused her hand at the slimness of her waist disallowing her a chance at sliding down her panties. "It's your call Nard." He glanced into her craving eyes and back down at her pubic area before sliding down the last piece of item over her thighs.

———————————————————

———————————————————

Nard drunken stature stumbled up the stairs fumbling with keys outside his door finding one that fit. A small family portrait on a nightstand went crashing to the floor where he slung the keys at. He tried quieting the commotion but added to its noise. Not a single light was on throughout the darken home staggering on through the living room. A bottle of Bom-Bay kept in the trunk for special occasions enhanced his earlier tipsy hoping to wash away any memories of what occurred at Lady's Luck tonight. A mistake he hoped would remain untold at all cost. He made it to the hallway bumping into something in its center aisle unable to distinguish it in the dark.

"Bernard, as long as I've known you you've never been this drunk. Why now?"

"Who-who dat'? Dats' you Tae'," words slurring. "Baby, come give daddy a, a huuuug." He reached out at her almost stumbling to the ground. "Where-where you at ... WUMAN'!"

"Bernard, is something wrong?"

"Yeeeeaah," regaining his posture, "YOU! Nex' question'."

"It's clear to me that you're talking out the side of your neck so I' think I'll be going back to bed. We'll finish this in the morning."

"Hell … I'm sleepy …too! Daddy kumin'!" He reached their room unable to turn to locked knob. "WU-MAN! I WUN' IN," pounding on the door. "YA' HEAR ME! I – I WUN' IN!"

"Daddy," lingering outside her bedroom door, "what's wrong?"

"SSSSSSSSHH! Yo' mutha' sleep. Go-go back to bed." She watched for the first time at her father careless behavior and closed the door. "I'M GONE WUMAN'! THAT'S RIGHT! GONE!"

He tried walking fast back down the hallway and pounced off the walls. Tripping over his feet, he landed face first on the floor. It wasn't long before the sounds of snoring accompanied him where he lay.

The water thrown on his face where he slept the remaining night awoken him to a new day. He wiped it dry identifying Shontae standing over him. It puzzled him as to why the living room floor was chosen for a place of rest unsure of yesterday's actions. In an instant, the thought of Peaches flashed through his mind praying he hadn't fell a victim to his old ways.

"What-what time is it?"

"Your late. I know that much."

"WORK!" He jumped up feeling dizzy. "Man! My head is throbbing. Fix me a glass of water and a couple Tylenols," sitting back down, head rested between his legs.

"Something isn't right Bernard. There's a cause behind your ignorance, and I will get to the bottom of it. Come on Asia." She grabbed hold of her daughter hand heading for the front door. "And by the way Mr. Hick, we will be discussing your problem later on today."

"What problem? I'm aiight'."

"No … you're not" departing the house.

"SHONTA-" massaging the pain in his head from yelling.

CHAPTER 13

"**M**ercedes Benz Dealership! How can I help you?"

"What it is pimpy!"

"ARE YOU CRAZY! What I told you bout' callin' me on my office phone?"

"Rexlax bra'. I got one word for you … JACKPOT!"

"You mean, jackpot as in, ka-ching'?

"Sho' you right."

He smothered the receiver with his hand peering out the office windows.

"I see you been on yo' job. That's a good thing."

"I was always taught that in order for a man to eat, you must always stay movin' yo' feet and most often, as swift as a horses ass."

"Aiight', aiight', here's the deal. You still owe me for transportation fee for the last drop-off."

"Just like you still owe me for several Mac-10's you left on yo' tab."

"I tell you what, lets call it even and start anew."

"Sounds like a plan to me."

"Location?"

"Uptown. On 13th Avenue. Third house. It's an ol' one with-"

"Hold up a second," placing the phone down, "COME IN!"

Sticking his head inside the office, "What's going on Mark."

"What's up Nard."

"One of your client was out here requesting of yo' services."

39

"Be out shortly. Preciate' it." He waited for the door to close placing the phone to his ear. "Now what were you sayen'?"

"Third house down the street from the Suga Shack. The hole-in-the-wall club in uptown."

"And the time?"

"It's a lil' after nine so I'll say," watching Trano whisper the time," 1 P.M."

"I'll be there. I'm out."

"Did you record all that John?"

"Got it Trano."

"Good! We gone need every bit of evidence for the D. A. to build its case and send him up the river for the rest of his life. You see how easy that was," spinning around in his chair facing the informant. "He didn't expect a thing. As soon as you mentioned money to him, he lost focus. Just that quick. A common mistake in this here new millennium. And you, my friend, have probably saved yourself from a long vacation away from your wife and kids."

"So why do I still feel like shit then?"

"That's normal for a rat or shall I say, a government informant."

He viewed the evil expression on Trano's face.

"And that's funny?"

"You damn right! But since you got so many questions how bout' answering this one." Trano chair slid directly up to his. "What do you think is gone happen to you if yo' man doesn't show for the pickup?" He had the slightest clue. "Let me have the honors in answering that for you then, that 8 by 10 you'll be hugging from dusk til' dawn for an eternity will not only grow colder and lonlier at night but those bed-bugs that bite, just don't try eaten' them like they're fish aiight'."

He sat motionless in close observation of Trano rearing back in the chair crossing his arms.

"You came in sort of staggering this morning. Rough night?"

"Very."

"I've had my share of those. Drove me into a drinking frenzy. Being sober had become so uncommon to me that I found myself waken' up in the driveway around six in the mornin'. Enough time to drag myself in, freshen up, get dress and be out before she had a chance to bore me with her jibberish. One helluva' life experience that was."

"What happen?"

"I go a divorce. What else! Went through rehabilitation and here I am. Back on top again and hay, I can't complain."

"Me neither. Not since I got that higher position several months ago. Things are much better at home. Well, at least until last night when I got too drunk to know I was drunk."

"Damn! Now that's being drunk."

"Don't forget to add in the foolish behavior that comes along with it."

"Oh boy. What you do?"

"Lets just say this, I awoke this mornin' to a raining shower on my face while laid out on the living room floor. Asleep! Wifey explained to getting to the bottom of it later on."

"I never knew you to be of the alcoholic type."

"I'm not. First and last time. That's for sure."

"Then it shouldn't be too hard in her forgiving you."

"You see, that's the problem Mark. I've erred in several other areas of our marriage. I mean, how much more can one take?"

"Mostly everything. Except infidelity."

"The one thing that can ruin everything."

The main reason behind his state of drunkenness last night. Spilling out old flames that lingered towards his son's mother should've remained a secret. Peaches wanting to be more involved with him didn't improve matters either. On top of that, his grandmother in serious condition at the hospital. Something he dread having to experience with her. Life had started to move faster than he could actually grab hold of and it bothered him deeply.

"Look here, I got to make a quick stop before I pick up our lunch. You cool with that?"

"Do yo' thang' man. I'm gone lay back and finish resting a lil'."

"Just right up her round' this corner. Looks like no," parking at the curb. "Give me a second. I'm go'en up to the door."

Nard hadn't moved a muscle. Too exhausted to try and identify his surrounding. It wasn't long before sleep had carried him over into a dream, apologizing to both his wife and daughter. She sat next to him on the bed embraced in his arm.

"Daddy acted real stupid last night Asia. The way I behave was irresponsible, foolish and out right stupid. I never meant to scare my lil' angel."

"Were you drunk daddy?"

"Yes," feeling embarrassed, "I was and I'm so sorry Asia."

"It's okay daddy. I still love you."

He felt relived she had forgiven him.

"But now it's my time to learn of the actual cause behind it all."

Shontae stood at the door awaiting for Nard to begin filling her in on every single detail.

"You mind if we go to our room. Away from our daughter."

"You need to hurry up then sir."

"Asia, thank you for being so understanding."

"No problem da-"

"TAP-TAP-TAP!"

The loud tapping sound on the window partially awoken him out his slumber noticing a shirt outside the window that read 'A.T.F.' in big letters.

"What the-"

Pulling open the passenger door, "Sir, you are under arrest for the trafficking of firearms."

"This some kind of joke, right," smiled Nard. "Aiight', aiight'. I'm gettin' punk'd. Okay, where the cameras at?"

Several other agents approached with their guns drawn.

"Sir, I'd advise you to step out of the car."

He looked around noticing Mark being escorted out a house in handcuffs.

CHAPTER 14

"**P**eaches, you been walkin' round' with a smile on yo' face since earlier this mornin'. Something I haven't seen in you since," pointing at her, "OOOOOOWEE! I know what it is! You done got you some aint' cha'? Yep! That's EXACTLY what it is! Why you horny lil' devil you. Care to fill me in."

"I'll say this Trish cause a real woman never tells her business but I'll give you a hint, he comes around every so often."

"That aint' tell'n me shit! All these men that be lined up outside the shop on a daily basis wantin a piece of yo' pie could be any one of them."

"Good afternoon ladies," stated Shannon upon having a seat.

"Someone got lucky last night."

"Trish, you late girl. As always. He came around-"

"Now stop right there miss. I was just sharing with her the importance of a lady refraining from sharing one's privacy."

"What's so private about that? Hell, ya'll already got one child together and looks like you might be workin' on a second one."

"So THAT'S the lucky man! But aint' he married though? I mean, couldn't that bring trouble Peaches? What if his wife finds out? You know how much ya'll two don't get along."

"Did any of ya'll ladies in here hear anything come out my mouth about sleeping with Nard?"

"Nah. No. Uh-uh," responded several occupants to her question.

"Okay then. Lets stop right here, right now with the untold truth and focus back on what's important and that's today. Not yesterday but today."

"Well, would you mind explaining to me why you were in such a rush in kickin' me out the shop last night? I couldn't even stay back and socialize with the young man for a minute. As soon as she finished my hair I was politely escorted out the front exit."

Shannon earned a position in the corporate world as a telemarketer. A single parent well equipt with taking care her daughter. Ten years into her marriage, she was forced to divorce her husband after receiving a STD (sexually transmitted disease). Thirty-five years of life hadn't displayed any sign of troubles on her face. Just a slender chin with high cheek bones partially covered by hair of an oily, perm distinction. Lips in resemblance to those of Stacy Dash. Skin tone a shade lighter. She weighed possibly twenty ponds more but fitted perfectly in her 5 foot 10' lengthy frame.

"Because you're to nosy Rosy. What you witnessed last night was a friendly visit by an individual making sure I was okay. His grandmother went into the hospital caused by a stroke and he needed someone to talk to."

"And hold. And squeeze. And … ladies, y'all know the rest," added Shannon. "But enough with all the extras cause all we want to know is did you or did you not enjoy yourself last night?"

The entire room went silent. She observed Shannon cross her leg in awaitance of an answer.

Opening her mouth to speak, "Yeeeees … he was the one to fix my stereo last night for me."

"AAAAAH NAH," voiced loudly the entire shop.

"He fine-tuned yo' radio aiight'," expressed Shannon. "Placed some plastic over his wire and plugged it into yo' socket."

"Isn't yo' boss callin' you Shannon? Aint' break over or something? Aren't you-"

"Headed out the door? Look here woman, this yo' last time kicki'n me out like this to. I'm grown. Just like you. I know how to find my way out this dump. Ladies, ya'll have a good day and as for you Mss. Peaches, just try not to short circuit where the plug loves workin. Chow!"

CHAPTER 15

"**O**FFICER! OFFICER!"

Nard sat next to Mark and many other criminals while in intake.

"Calm down young man. I'll get to you in a minute. Just cause you cute and all don't mean you get any special treatment from me."

"Officer, you don't understand. I need to pick my son up from school."

"He got a mother don't he"

"Of course but she doesn't know I'm here."

"You'll get to make a call shortly but for now, chill-out a minute cause we'll soon be proceedin' with dressin y'all out. And by the way, welcome to the cesspool."

The dark-skin, heavy-set woman stationed behind the counter found her normal greeting to newly arrived inmates funny. Her chipped nails and undone hair proved appearance was at the bottom of her list nor any lipstick to cover the dry skin pealing loose on her large lips.

"Man! I can't BELIEVE I'm in here! All from hangin' out with yo' ass."

"Just relax, aiight'. Let me figure this thing out."

"FIGURE IT OUT," snapped Nard rising to his feet. "NIGGA', IF YOU DON'T CLEAR MY NAME OF THIS BULL-"

"OR WHAT," standing up to him. "WHAT YO' ASS GONE DO!"

"SAY WHAT! MUTH-" taking a swing at Mark's head. His fist landed on a cheek slitting it open before they tumbled down across several chairs.

"GUARDS TO ASSIT FIGHT IN INTAKE! GUARDS TO ASSIST FIGHT IN INTAKE," repeating in her walkie-talkie for assistance. "BREAK IT UP YOU TWO! BREAK IT UP!"

Numerous of officers burst through the door slamming them both down.

The lieutenant watched off from a distance mentioning, "Put the cuffs on them two clowns and get them down to a holdin' tank. Now!

CHAPTER 16

H ave a seat Mrs. Hick. Take a load off of your feet."

"Thanks."

"How are we feeling today?"

"Not to good."

"Oh! And why is that?"

"My husband."

"You mean that wonderful piece of sculpture you have at home?"

"If that's what you prefer to call him."

"And what seems to be the problem?"

"Last night, for the very first time in our relationship, he came home.... drunk."

"And his behavior?"

"Stupid foolish."

"My! Was there some recent problem or differences between you two?"

"No. Not at all."

"How bout' family issues? Work issues? You know, things of that nature?"

"Not to my knowledge."

"The reason why I ask these questions is because most of our actions are reactions caused by a lingering issue or a problem. His day-to-day normal routine didn't cause it but something or someone pushed his behavior over the edge. Now, what I'd advise you to do is to be patient with him coming forth about the situation. Let him bring it to you first. Let his conscious way in on him to the point where it'll possibly worry him senseless. Maybe even crazy. Well, not actually crazy but you get my point. Just go on living your normal life. Remain on a positive path and allow the past to either rest or resolve itself. Life effects us all differently. Most of us in a negative way due to a lack of constructive habits. In other words, be who you are. Control your emotions. Let wasted thoughts destroy themselves. Prosper on blessings shared and blessings earned.

"Sometimes, I find myself very frustrated with the world. You know, with my father not being here. That sort of adds on to the pain I'm already experiencing with in my life. I mean, it's hard."

"Have you asked yourself how you've been able to maintain your sanity for this long?

"Not really."

"The answer is already within you. You practice it every day. Even when you were a kid and remained confined to your room shortly after your father's loss you was grooming yourself for something most adults doesn't even possess today. I'll give you a clue: It practice it in his movement and is best known for beating a rabbit to the finish line."

"What …. A turtle!"

"And what does a turtle practice in his actions?"

"Taking his sweet time in getting from point A to B?"

"Right! Patience. So you see there was plenty gain from a misfortune. They say everything happens for a reason but I believe reasons come about to establish the true strength and weaknesses of a person character. You've proven your strength. Now desist with your weaknesses cause as far as I'm concern, you have none. Be thankful for who you are. The key to it all is simple: Pace your stride and slow your mind! A major factor in anyone maintaining their sanity."

"Ain't that the truth."

The visits always offered her a better insight in life. A sense of relief. Time away from hardships. Something she struggled with in the past five years. Especially after taking on the responsibility in raising another child that meant having to deal with her nemesis which, at times, drew the line. She kept the therapist a secret from Nard only making random visits in hopes of him never finding out. The last thing she wanted to do was give him the impression a problem might've occurred that they couldn't resolve together but she needed someone other than him to confide in.

"How you feeling momma?"

"A lot betta'. That's fa'sure."

"I told you about standing over that hot stove so much. You had a grandson in their willing to do anything we asked of him to do?"

"Believe me child, it wasn't in my plan to cause pain on myself but whatever the Lord has in store for us, theirs pretty much nuthin' we can do about it except roll with the punches. I still can feel a lil' pain in my chest. I bet you the doctor put all sorts of drugs in me. I asked him how much longer they were gone keep me and he said he was uncertain. And where is lady fur? Who's lookin' after her?"

"She's fine momma'. I been stayin' at your place makin' sure no one trys to vandalise it. As for you getten' out, we'll just have to wait and see. It's only been a week. Maybe no more than one week of this and you'll be home before you know it."

"I sure hope you right. My garden need tending to. The neighborhood kids need a yard to play in. I enjoy watchin' them run around having fun on my spacious yard."

"Calm down momma'. You're getting' too worked up here. Save some of that energy. Everything is gonna' work itself out."

CHAPTER 17

"**W**ell, well, well," approaching Nard's cell. Phone in hand. "Looks like you do receive special treatment from me after all. PHONE SERVICE! She unlocked the flap to his door placing the phone atop of it.

"Thank you mamm. You just don't know how much I appreciate this. If their's anything I can do for you once I'm freed, just let me know."

Her head bent downward close to the slot whispering, "Honey, I would love to show you off on my arm at Ben's Wings and Things one Friday night enjoyin' a nice plate of chicken wings and fries."

He placed a hand over his mouth trying to refrain from laughing in her face.

"Miss, you got that."

"Stay out of trouble sexy. I'll be back shortly."

———————————————————————

———————————————————————

"The boy has been out of the house long enough Shenequa. How much longer you plan on maken' our only child survive on his own in the jungle? It could get very hectic for him you know."

"Until I see blood flood the whites of his eyes. You actin' like it's been

50

several months or something. Let me find out you done got soft on me already."

"Not hardly woman." He was very concern of M-J's safety but kept it hidden from her. "But what sense does it make to keep draggin' him in the mud like this? I think he might've learned his lesson."

"Well, I don't think so. Next topic please."

"Me getten' a lil' bit of that good ol' luvy'-luv' of yours."

"How bout' you luvy-luvin' yo' self in the bathroom down the hall. All the privacy you need."

"Oh Lord! Not this again. Look here, I an't in the mood for fighten' right now and I definitely ain't in the mood for no ejaculation. My hand starten' to get calluses on it from giving myself the special treatment to much."

"Quit squeezing it so hard. I'll be aiight'."

"We ain't got that much time left before we're back off to work. A quickie would be lovely right about now."

"You really want some of this nukie' Mike? Do you?"

"And you know this …. MAAAAN!"

"How you want it then? You want it like this," sliding off the couch onto her hands and knees on the floor. Excitememt flashed across his eyes. "From the back? Or how bout' I lay on my back?" She laid out flat. Legs extended apart. "You like it? Nah, nah. You the spoil type. I know what you want. You want it in my mouth don't you? Yeah. That's exactly what daddy wants'."

"Girl, you learning more and more about yo' man every day."

She unloosen his zipper. Pants and boxer pulled down to his knees grabbing hold of his erection. Her mouth now aimed for his phallus.

"That's it baby girl. Cocked, aimed and ready to explode."

His erection just inches away from her widen mouth mentioning, "Damn Mike! I almost forgot."

"WHA-WHAT'! FORGOT WHAT," frustrated with her sudden stoppage.

"My toothe ache honey," standing to her feet. "Maybe some other time."

She faded out down the hallway.

"I …. BE…DAMN! Can you believe this-"

'ARE YOU GONNA' ANSWR THE PHONE," shouting from out their bedroom.

"DAMN THAT PHONE! ARE YOU GONE GIVE ME SOME HEAD IS WHAT I WANNA' KNOW!"

"YEAH! AS SOON AS YOU GET IT EXAMINED!"

"Maaan, this woman trippin'," mumbling to himself. "She worried bout' some damn phone. I'm tryen' to get some head. Sittin' here half naked and shit-HELLO!"

"You have a collect call from … Bernard Hick. To accept the call, press 5 now. To deny this call, press-"

"Hello."

"What in the world are you doing callin' me from the county jail bra'?"

"We'll get into all that a lil' later cause I only got a few minutes of phone time. But I need you to get in touch with momms' and wifey after you hang up with me and have them find a bondsman to post bail and get me out of her A.S.A.P."

"You ain't gotta' say no mo'. Do me a favor though?"

"And what's that?"

"Keep the soap on a tight rope when you and the shower water float down stream together."

"Ha … ha … ha."

"Just a lil' humor to try and brighten' up things until we can get you out of there. I'm gone."

CHAPTER 18

Shontae hadn't to long walked out the office before receiving a call from Mike of Nard's incarceration. The news almost forced her to return back inside and remain hidden only to never be seen in society again. She sat awhile inside her car. Vexed. Baffled. Uncertain of what her tomorrow might possibly bring into fruition. He instructed her of contacting Ms. Hick on the phone but to no avail. Deciding to drop by her place seem the only option left. The driveway displayed no sight of any transportation. Thirty-minutes was long enough to await her arrival and afterwards, she would proceed in trying to free her husband with or without anyone help. Ms. Hick shortly arrived pulling up beside her on side of the curb.

Rolling down her window, "My, this is a surprise! How's my daughter-in-law doing these days?"

"Not so good."

"And why is that? Is something wrong?"

"Yes! Nard is in jail."

"IN JAIL!"

"I not to long ago got a call from Mike and he said for us to get a bondsman to bail him out. He said he'll meet us there."

"What in the world has this boy done gotttin' himself into this time? I tell you the truth! If it ain't one thing it's another on God's green earth. Well, come on and follow me then."

Ms. Hick wondered how serious of trouble her son was in. A location she knew him to never had visit in his entire life. She wanted her middle child home by any means even if it meant putting up every single thing she owned. Prison was one location she wished of no one to ever have to experience but some acts were beyond forgiving and she hoped his trouble was far from it.

CHAPTER 19

"**P**eaches! Peaches," yelling over the commotion, "you got some type of collect call on your phone? You want me to accept it?"

"What's it sayin' Trish?"

"Something bout' a collect call from a Bernard Hick."

She placed the hot curler in her hand on the counter top rushing to retrieve it.

"Let me see that Trish. Hello!" The recorded voice repeated itself a second time pressing five. "Nard!"

"What's up Peaches?"

"Where you at!"

"That's what I call to talk to you about."

"About what? Nard, what's goin' on?"

"You have to go pick our son up from school. I'm in a lil' jam."

"What kind of jam? You in some type of trouble?"

"I got arrested."

"Are you serious!"

"Dead serious."

"What you need for me to do? Come pick you up?"

"Nah'. I got in touch with Mike and he gone take care of everything for me.

I just need you to pick our son up cause I'm runnin' a lil' late."

"AIIGHT' SEXY," alerted the constable walking toward his cell. "Your phone time is up! I done spoiled you long enough."

55

"I gotta' go Peaches."

"That sounds like some lady in the background. Who is that Nard."

"Big Shirley."

"Big Shirley?"

"A female officer. Look, just go get our son as soon as you hang up. I'll see you in a lil' while."

"How soo" –hearing the dial tone.

"Was that your baby-daddy?"

"Yes it was."

"What he doin' in jail?"

"How you know where he's at?"

"I got a cousin who's always callin' my mother a lot from the county jail."

"Wow. That's not good at all but here's what I need for you to do."

"Talk to me boss lady."

"You have to hold the shop down for me for a while. An emergency done came up."

"I got you."

"Here's your first shot at runnin' Lady's Luck for us. I believe you can handle it." She grabbed a couple of her personal belongings and sped for the door. Stopping at the exit, "Don't let me down Trish."

"Don't worry yourself. I said I got you. Now go handle yo' business."

Something Peaches couldn't stop worrying about while en route to her son's school. Nard's arrest came as a shock knowing about his past history of never experiencing any run-ins with the law. Her gut feeling informed her of it all being some type of mixup. A mistaken identity. D.W.B. (Driving While Black). Possibly a police seeking some sort of revenge for recognizing Nard as the one sleeping with his wife in the past. Anything except him actually committing a crime. His responsibility as a man and toward his family was all that mattered and she highly respected him for it.

The school parking lot displayed a handful of transportation still remaining. A long haired white boy rode on a bike back and forth in front of the entrance. Peaches continued viewing the area identifying her son know where. Exiting the building with a suitcase held firmly in her grasp, Ms. Drew, his homeroom teacher, headed in her direction.

Stepping out her parked car, "Excuse me, Ms. Drew?"

"Yes," coming to a stop.

"How are you mamm? I'm runnin' a lil' late in picking my son up but I don't see him anywhere. I was wondering have you seen him recently or is he possibly still inside?

"And what is your son's name?"

"Kedar Fifer mamm."

"I knew you looked familiar! You own that beauty shop called Lady's Luck. I've been there a couple of times before. Y'all do nice work there too."

"Thank you mamm." She wasn't the least bit interest in small talk but in finding her baby and making it back to the shop. "But is he in there?"

"No. Not at all. School been over almost forty-five minutes now. Maybe he might've left with a friend."

"Would you happen to know who that friend might've been?"

"I sure don't young lady. Sorry."

"Thank you for your time mamm."

She rehearsed with Kedar more than a hundred times in the past on calling her first when an emergency occurred. Contacting him on the phone she purchased for such occasion proved futile. Maybe he left it at home on his dresser or rode with a friend and was too busy to answer it. "What if he was abducted?" Negative thoughts flooded her mind. She started to panic. A situation no parent would ever want to experience with their child. The recreation park he played at a block away from their home was crowded with children enjoying themselves and still, no sign of him. The tears swelling in her eyes were clear signs of doubts. Uncertainty. Fearful of his whereabouts. Her speedy return back to the shop somehow managed to evade a patrolmen from furthering her problems.

"PLEASE," plopping down in a chair, "somebody help me! I can't find my baby!"

'Yeah you can momma," exiting the bathroom. "Here I am."

"OH MY BABY!" She rushed to where he stood dropping down to her knees. "Are you alright? How did you get here?"

"One of his friends dropped him off Peaches," answered Trish.

"And all this time I been out here lookin' for my baby. How come you ain't call me Trish?"

"You didn't quite exactly inform me where you were going. Plus, I been kind of busy holdin' the shop down."

"Thank you for the extra help Trish. You did good. And as for you young man, where's your phone at?"

"It's over there! In my bag." He went and searched the side pocket where he keep it at. "See," holding it up. "I told you I had it." The three-inch screen was void of any writing. "Uh-oh!

"Uh-oh what?"

"That's why I didn't hear you. It's been off."

"Well, it doesn't even matter now. As long as you are in one piece, mommy is okay.

But what I told you about contacting me to let me know when something is wrong?"

"When daddy didn't show up, my friend mother asked if I was okay and I told her my daddy was runnin' a lil' late. She offered me a ride so I said yeah. Where is daddy mommy?"

"He -," choosing her words wisely, "he had a minor accident with his car."

"Is he alright," showing deep concern.

"He's alright … I hope."

She wasn't sure just how much trouble he was in. All she knew that he was in jail and could only hope for his immediate return. In one piece.

CHAPTER 20

"**O**kay everyone, here's the deal. I went over to the jail, enquired about your son bail and their exact words were, 'No can do!' He has to go through some type of hearing from the judge in order to be granted bond. They said something about the severity of his offense being a serious one. I'm sorry Ms. Hick'"

"Exactly how serious is his offense sir," she questioned.

"Gun trafficking."

'GUN TRAFFICKING! Oh my God. I need a seat." Mike slid a chair up close noticing her giddiness. "Thank you son. Did you just say gun trafficking? Are you sure that was my son you went and asked about?"

"Bernard Hick's ain't it?"

"Yep. That's him. This has to be some kind of mistake sir. My son has never committed a crime a day in his life. So how long are we talkin' bout' waitin' before this hearing takes place?"

"Days. Weeks. Maybe a few months. Depends on his mood."

"So you mean to tell me that if the judge is having a bad day, my son is in for a long stay?"

"Pretty much."

"Ain't this bout a bi-"

"Take is easy Ms. Hick," intervened Mike. "Let me speak with him a minute. Excuse me sir, what type of foolishness are you talkin' about' here? My partna' is locked up on some hum-bug that I know he didn't do and you sayin' we have to wait for some judge to hopefully wake up to a good day? Can I say something and please, don't take this to offensive sir but you sound crazy as hell."

"Hey, don't blame me. I'm just the middle-man."

"And you're doing a piss-poor of a job at it too," commented Shontae. "It's only one judge? Isn't their other ones?"

"Yes there are but only one for bond hearings. If you folks don't mind, I need to make an important call in my office. Stay as long as you like but please be sure to lock the door behind you."

Ms. Hick wanted badly to inflict pain on the lanky man but was more afraid his delicate limbs would break in half. Mike paced the floor angered at how the bondsman was of no use. The thought of Nard surrounded by weirdo disturbed him. He wondered how well his friend would manage until he was freed.

"So what do we do now," asked Shontae.

"Their's really not much we can do except wait on the judge," explained Ms. Hick. "Until then, we go on with our day-to-day lives and hope the judge wake up with the sun shinen' on his ashy forehead."

"That's easy for you to say. He has some important duties to attend to at home. What am I suppose to tell our daughter that her father is in jail?"

"Not exactly. Stretch the truth a lil'. You know, a friendly white lie. Tell her daddy and his boss went out of town on a unexpected business trip."

"And you think she'll believe that?"

"I don't see why not. Kids are easy to deceive. Whenever he calls home to talk to you, be sure you let her hear his voice. She'll eventually settle herself down some about his absence."

"I sure hope you're right Ms. Hick's."

CHAPTER 21

"**M**-J!"

"Yeah coach."

"After this scrimmage play, let me speak with you for a minute off to the side if you don't mind."

"Sure coach." The entire time while out on the field, he wondered what Coach Jones might've wanted to converse about. No one knew of his stay at Johny Blocka' residence except his friend parents who possibly shared it with others. The recorded coitus was locked away safely in his trunk enclosed in a lockbox wasting no further energy entertaining the thought of what to do with it next. He trotted over to where his coach was in conversation.

"What's up," catching his breath, "Coach."

"Give me a second with the boy Coach Thomas." He waited for the two were alone spitting some snuff out his mouth on the ground. "Son, now I've known you for quite some time now. I even followed your performance all through junior high school but something is different about your skills on the field over the past week that's deeply bothering me. You rushed for your lowest yardage ever our last game. Now usually when a kid performance isn't at its best that's a clear sign that their's a problem. Is it girl problems son?"

Laughing at his comment, "Definitely not that Coach."

"How bout' family then? Is everything aiight' at home?"

"I guess so. Yeah"

"You sure? You don't sound to convincing there."

"I'm straight Coach but thanks for your concern. Is it aiight' if I go in for this play they're about to run?"

"Go right ahead son but if something is ailing you, ANTHING, don't be afraid to let it off your chest. Consult with me if need be."

He felt relieved Coach knew nothing of his scenario at home. The crawling sounds of rats heard throughout most the night deprived him of any decent rest and his tiredness was starting to display itself out on the field. He didn't know how much longer he could continue living in what seem like a dungeon. Shenequa continued denying any contact with him. His father tried pleading with her but was useless.

"That boy is the best player on our team Coach."

"I know that. Whatever it is bothering him is definitely hindering his performance."

"I overheard a few of the players say he's homeless. Living with our starting offensive lineman Mr Johny Blocka' Blockingdale."

Glimpsing at his defensive coordinator, "Which would explain everything. The boy has great parents! I know them personally. He must've done something awful bad. I think I'll head over to pay them a visit. You know, sort of get to the bottom of it."

CHAPTER 22

Nard dozed off for almost an hour awakening to an unfamiliar place. A single blanket covered only three-fourths of his body which he struggled with fighting off the freezing temperatures. His bare feet in shower shoes the county jail had issues him felt numb. The ceiling extended around fifteen feet from off the ground appearing further from where he rested on a torn cot. His captivity reminded him of a caged bird awaiting for its owner failure in securing the door for a possible escapage.

A window out of arms reach permitted a minor portion of daylight that was converting over into the night darkening his cell. He trusted Mike had informed his family of his conditions. What delayed his release was uncertain and he began pacing the floor. A shrill, howling sound disturbed the peaceful corridor. Inmates pounding on doors pursed next.

The dangling sound of keys quieted the commotion. Nard approached the door peering through a narrow slit in desperate search of anyone. An officer continued walking pass his cell. Pain struck his heart. Sadden at his chance of freedom fading fast. Incarcerated for the wrongful act of another man. "But why me, God," posing the question aloud.

BERNARD NICK!" He leaped up off the bunk and hurried to view out the window. PACK IT UP! YOU GO'EN TO POPULATION!"

"Population," hearing the door unlock.

"Grab all your stuff issued to you."

"I ain't got nothing really. They just put me in here a couple hours or so ago for fightin'."

"Fightin' you say? Oh, you gonna' love where you're headed then."

"I'm goin' into population right? Back to the streets. That is what you meant?"

"Bad news commando! I was given strict orders to take you upstairs on the fifth floor. The Thunder Dome!"

"What about my bond?"

"What about it? Yo' hearing probably won't be reviewed by the judge for several weeks. Minimum."

"WEEKS!"

The officer placed him in a set of handcuffs behind his back and escorted him down the long hallway.

"That's right. Weeks. Or possibly months."

"You got to be kiddin' me. But I didn't do nuthin'!"

"Sure you didn't but join the rest of the one thousand and some inmates already here claiming their innocence."

CHAPTER 23

"Hello Mrs. Turner."

"Hello Coach Jones. What brings you by?"

"The future success of your talented son on and off the field."

"You know how he is. He loves himself some football. Come on in couch. Have a seat on the couch. Would you like anything to drink or eat?"

"No mamm. I'm fine. Thank you. I didn't mean to drop by so late in the evening unannounced."

"That's okay. Me knowing you as the business man you are, it has to be something of great importance."

"Yes, it is. Your son's performance on the field is the worst I've ever seen it. He clearly stated to me that everything is alright at home and that girl problems is irrelevant. My reason for being here today is to ask you have you seen any sudden change in his behavior? Some sign of trouble he might be experiencing in the community?"

"Not that I can remember. He appeared to be himself lately but this my first time hearing of his troubles on the field."

"You mean he hasn't consulted with you about it?"

"No. Not at all."

"That's strange. As much as you and his father used to attend his game. If I can recall, you used to be his loudest fan."

"That's before Junior became a senior."

"I'm not quite understanding you."

"Coach Jones, we experienced an incident a while back. A very bad one. One that forced our son to find a place of his own."

"You mean, he moved out?"

"No. Kicked out!"

"But he's such a great kid! Very discipline."

"Until he understands the true meaning of what discipline is, he's right where he belongs. Somewhere in the world doing what grownups do."

"Mamm, I'm not here to tell you how to raise your son-"

"So don't," cutting his statement short.

"I'll share something with you mamm if you don't mind and afterwards, find the nearest exit. My mother once told me when I was a child that a mistake is something we all make but when it's done twice then that's when the mistake has grown into a problem and the only way to cure a problem is by letting the problem face itself. He knows he was wrong and I can assure you the pain is evident. His youth is his only real advantage in life right now but if you take that away from him, you'll regret it in the end. Lets just be thankful he hasn't reached the ages of thirty-five or forty when the damage could've been more detrimental causing him to possible lose out on everything. Think about it Mrs. Turner," Picking up his western sombrero off beside him. "Have a good night mamm."

She didn't mean to offend him by interrupting his comment but her decision had already been finalized and it made no sense discussing anything further about it. Mike entered through the front door not long after Coach had departed.

"Was that Junior coach leaving out the driveway? What did he want? Something wrong with our son? He's in more trouble ain't he? You see! See what I been tellin' you!"

"Calm down grasshoppa'. There's nothing wrong with your grown-child. The coach stopped by informing me how M-J's performance on the field has dropped tremendously."

"Naaaah? Are you serious," enquired sarcastically. "I wonder why."

"You got jokes don't you?"

"Nah. YOU got jokes by makin' a mockery of our boy. You might wanna' put some serious consideration in allowing him back home before something bad really happens to him."

"Let me sleep on it. That's a mistake I just can't get over that easy. I'm sure I never will. I mean, what the hell he was thinkin'?"

"That's the problem. He wasn't."

"You think his is now?"

"I should hope so."

"Like I said, I'll sleep on it and that's it. He just betta' hope I don't have a bad dream or that's his ass."

"Someone else dreams are probably doing bad as we speak. Nard is in jail and they wouldn't even allow him a bond."

"GET THE HELLOUT OF HERE! You mean Mr. Perfect is in the slammer! Fo' what?

You know his butt ain't in to the crime life. I bet he's goin' crazy up there aint' he?"

"I don't know. He didn't sound to bothered about the scenario over the phone."

"What he supposedly do?"

"They got him for gun trafficking."

"Was he about to go to war with somebody?"

"Not that I know of. Wrong place and time is all I can think of."

"Let me know if you need my help for anything but right now, I'm goin' to bed.

It's singles night."

"What the hell is that?"

"Where I sleep alone and you sleep out here. You do want me to have a good night of sleep don't you?"

"Of course but I think I can make it a lil' bit better for you."

"Junior is gonna' be very mad at you if he found out you wasn't lettin' mommy get any good rest on makin' her decision. Enjoy you're night."

He didn't even bother putting up a fight. Too exhausted from trying to free his right hand man from a place depriving a person of privacy, loved ones and most importantly, FREEDOM! Tomorrow he would get a better start in finding a way to get him out of there or protest in front of the building for his friend great return.

CHAPTER 24

"Sir …. Sir! Excuse me sir?" The officer ignored her for the most part signaling to wait. Ms. Hick calmly sat back down. She had arrived at 7:30 in the morning. Shontae accompanied her. Weekend visiting hours started in thirty minutes. A handful of visitors lingered in the waiting room for the same reason. On different attempts she questioned how soon it would be before seeing her son, and no one gave her a forward answer. The time on her wrist stated fifteen minutes after ten. The building was packed with very little moving space. She witnessed some who arrived after her escorted through double doors for their visits. "Enough is Enough!" Politeness never seem to work in her favor and decided to ante up the stakes. "Shontae, this won't take nuthin' but a minute."

"What you about to do Ms. Hick," holding her back at the arm.

"Just relax. I got this," making her way through the crowd. She repeatedly pound a fist on the fiber glass window that separated her from the officers. Her mouth placed up to the slot yelling, "IF DON'T NOBOBY POINT ME IN THE RIGHT DIRECTION TO SEE MY SON, I'M GOIN' OFF IN HERE AND IT WON'T BE ONE HICK YOU'LL HAVE LOCKED UP BUT TWO BY THE TIME I FISHISH!" He pointed to a door on her right. "See how easy that was," looking back at the silenced room. "Thank you sir. Come on Shontae.!"

"Yo' celly! You can't sleep it all away," entering their two-man cell. "Go play cards or something. You been in here a week and I can count on one hand the times you been outside this cell. You don't eat. Don't watch T.V. It is what it is in here play boy! But at the way you're doin' it it's gonna' do more harm in the end. This your first time ever being locked up ain't it? And you said you was how old?"

Mumbling from underneath his pillow, "Thirty-six."

"So you one of them dudes that had it made all your life?"

"Because of never being in this place?" Nard sat up on the top bunk. "Not hardly bra'. I grew up poorer that the other kids in my neighborhood. It might've looked as if we had money because of all the nice houses that surrounded us but come to find out, we lived in a house so small that even when the rats crept in and out they used to tap us on the leg sayen', "Excuse me sir, you mind if I can get by.'"

"Damn! Now that's small."

"So yeah, I know more about the struggle than you could imagine but it was reading that kept my mind preoccupied on something constructive and off the foolishness that went on around me. I ended up at Clarke University and in the process, became a professional at selling cars for Mercedes Benz which accumulated plenty money for me. But now I'm locked up. In jail! Fo' nuthen'," plopping his head down onto the pillow.

"I feel you on that but no need to continue cryin' over spill milk. Just try and make the best of a bad situation."

"That's easy for you to say. You been here almost two years."

"And still countin'. It is what it is with mines. My days of freedom are over. I'm lookin' at hard times for the rest of my life." J-Dub stared at his face in a square piece of stainless steel screwed into the wall wondering what identity of his looked back at him. "But it's all good though. Whoever said life was sweet. Some of us has to kill to eat on them evil streets. I worked too hard trying to establish my empire. Along with my dearest friend from the past. May you rest in peace 2-Piece." He eyed to the sky stirring up deep distress over the loss of someone he considered his only true brother. "You know, they don't make them like us no more. Too much fake shit in the game. The so-call big-boy out there is the same one given up names. How can you win?"

"You can't. That's why I never participated in it. But why you didn't try legalizin' all the money you made? Why continue gamblin' with your life like that? It doesn't make any sense."

"It does when all you have is an eight-grade education. Trust me, I wanted to do that AND some but I didn't know how to go about communicating nor present myself in the corporate world. So me being so knee-deep in the streets, that made the dream of it all fade itself out more in my sleep at night."

Several knocks on the closed door quickly gained their attention. J-Dub signaled at the man to enter.

"Excuse me fellas', which one of y'all Bernard Hick's?"

"That'll be me my man," raising up.

"They callin' you up front for a visit."

"Good lookin'," jumping down off the bunk.

"Well killah', go get you some air. Go show your people that you're handling yo' situation like the man you are."

"Thank you for the prep talk celly."

"Anytime Nard. Anytime," viewing him depart through the dorm front door.

"You two can have a seat at the fourth booth to your left," smacking on her gum.

"Use your time wisely ladies."

"One hour is all you ladies have! Use it wisely! I should use that wig of hers wisely for a mop head."

"She's only doin' her job Ms. Hick."

"That's the problem. She AIN'T doin' her job. Wastin' all her time sittin' on that fat-"

"Hey!"

"There's yo husband." Nard took a seat on the stool grabbing hold of the phone.

"Hello son."

"Hi mom'."

"How my baby doin'?"

"Just tyrin' to adjust to such," looking around at the all metal and brick room, "an ugly place."

"You can handle it. God wouldn't have put you through this if he known you wasn't strong enough to endure it."

"Amen to that."

"As for your bond hearing being denied Thursday, we gotta just pray for the best and prove your innocence in the court. We went out and got you a lawyer as much as I hate to hear how that sound."

"The judge said I was a risk factor. Can you believe that? I never broke the law. Not even a traffic ticket."

"I know son. Blame it on the devil in a robe. You know how these people are in the south. The only thing they respect about us is nothing."

"What about the lawyer? He wasn't too expensive was he?"

"Not enough to hurt that large bank account of you and your lovely wife," smiled Ms. Hick.

"You're a wonderful mother momma'. How's grandma? You explained to her of my condition?"

"I'm not gonna' worry her yet with it. Let her continue to rest a lil' longer and we'll go from there but let me give this phone to your wife. Don't forget to say your prayers at night. I love you son."

She hurried away from the booth shielding her pain, refusing to weaken at the sight of her child horrible conditions.

"Hay baby."

"You know I'm innocent? You do believe me don't you?"

"Yes baby. I believe you."

"Wrong place, wrong time with the wrong person. But we've been coworkers for years! How was I suppose to know he was transporting illegal firearms while using Mercedes vehicles. He seemed innocent to me. Or at least he never talked about doing anything wrong in my presence. Occasionally, a few stops were made at some run-down houses between some of the errands I rode with him on in the company car but that was it. I figured they were relatives."

"Sounds to me like you wasn't to aware of your surrounding. Nor friends. So what me and Asia suppose to do now with you in here? What if they refuse to let you out any time soon? My career can only foot so much of the bills."

"We got enough money in the bank that'll hold us down for a while. Definitely until I'm freed."

"And exactly when is that suppose to be? I did a lil' research on the offense they charged you with and it carries a minimum of thirty-six months. Aiding and abetting."

"He sent word that he was going to free me as soon as possible. Tell the courts I had no type of involvement."

"And if he doesn't? What then? What if he say you was an accomplice?"

"There is no WHAT IF! Look, the man is aiight' with me. He'll do the right thing."

"I can't tell! He left you in the blind about this which ended you here behind this-this three-inch glass dressed in a dingy blue jump suit that reads Muscogee County Jail on it. Nard, baby, you need to wake up and fast. We need you at home."

"I need for you to relax and stay focused until this drama quickly blows over." Their eyes locked in on each other. Not a word spoken. He rested a hand flat on the glass. She mimicked his move. "Shontae?"

"Bernard?"

"You love me?"

"Did not I say 'I do'?"

"Did not I say 'I will'?"

She blew him a kiss,

"TIMES UP PEOPLE," yelled the guard.

"I gotta' go baby."

"Okay. Be careful in their Nard."

"Tell my angel face daddy loves her. Put my momma back on the phone right quick."

She grew teary eyed handing Ms. Hick the phone.

"I love you," she whispered from behind his mother.

"Momma', you be easy out there until I get home. Try and keep that bull-headed temper of yours down some for me. Can you do that?"

"You know how your mother do things. One minute I'm relaxed and the next, I'm ready to kick off in somebody tail."

"Trust me, I already know."

"If it's anything you need son, please give me a call. I'm praying for you."

"Tell them brothas' of mine I said I'm holding up pretty good. I gotta' go. I love you woman."

"Bye son! TAKE CARE," shouting from behind the glass. She watched them place a set of handcuffs on his wrist and walk him out through a large metal door.

CHAPTER 25

"I'm out there on the field busten' my ass almost every day of the week for you! Putten' dudes on they back. Makin' you a hole wide enough that a mack truck can even pass through and now, all of a sudden, you wanna' lag in your performance as if you don't care any mo'. We got a big game in one week. What's up dawg'? You aiight?"

"You bout' the fifth person to ask me that."

"All that mean is that they see the same problem with you that I do. Maybe you done got home sick. Is that what it is? You wanna' stop by mommy house? Does mommy need to give her baby a great big huuuuuuug?"

"No need. I got you for all that." Johny Blocka' wasn't the least bit thrilled with his friend answer. "To be honest, feel like I'm startin' to lose interest in the game. I'm gettin' older J-B. I mean, who's to say I might make it to a good college off a scholarship. That shit ain't promise you know."

"I know that ain't you talken' like that. No way dawg'! Can't believe it! Not the kid who had a baby bottle made into a football. This been yo' thang' since the ages of time. You can tell that lie to someone who don't know you."

"People change. Maybe I have to."

"Definitely not you. Maybe someone incapable of steppin' they game up but certainly not Carter G. Woodson High School greatest."

"A few things has been bothering me these last couple of days. Like the crazy looks yo' mother been sharin' with me lately. That's not a good sign at all big homie'."

"She asked me the other day rather you plan on stayin' forever and if so, she was gone request that you pay a bill around the house."

"Pretty strong stipulation for such a short stay ain't it?"

"Two weeks and counting? You do the math."

"I guess I have to respect that and get on some type of grind. Maybe even get a job." He never worked a day in his life and didn't know how or where to actually begin in search of one. The few dollars he survived on was nearing an end. A call to his dad for more might last him another week or so and afterwards, find a better means for survival. He contemplated on several different ideas for coming up with a solution. Parked on the driveway of his friend home is an important piece of material destine to bring in enough currency to last him for as long as he needed. "Why didn't I think of that earlier?"

"Think of what?"

"The precious item stored away in my trunk. That's something that'll definitely rake in plenty dough."

"I don't know M-J. We had this discussion before. That's a plan I'm totally against. Think smart homeboy before you start to make your life harder than what it already is."

"Oh, my mind is made up. The next step is finding a location to allow close observation of what I'm workin' with."

Johny Blocka' expressed disdain but out of respect for his friend, chose to go with the flow.

"You wanna' check out a few corners to see if anyone wants part of this?"

"Waste of time. Not enough money on them streets for me. I'm looken' for that hollywood bread and what better place to start at then the freakiest place on earth?"

"You talken' bout' a strip club?"

"Not by far my big-foot friend. How bout a porno shop."

"But which one?"

"ALL of them! Or at least until I come up with the best hook-up."

CHAPTER 26

"It took you long enough to come see me."

"Boy please! You the one who sent the visiting form almost two weeks after your arrest."

"How's my son?"

"He's aiight'. Handling it like the young man he's growin' up to be."

"It's kind of hard tryin' to talk to him over the phone like this. You know, hearing the concern in his voice wondering where I'm at and if I'm coming home soon."

"Well, are you?"

"At this point, I don't even know. My former co-worker aint' even responding back to the messages I keep sending him. I got a lawyer visit coming up this week. It looks as if, for now, I gotta' play it by ear."

"So you don't know what's goin' on?"

"Basically."

"If it makes you feel any better, here's where I stand with it all, no matter how long it takes for your return, I'm definitely gonna' be here for you."

"Are you really?"

"Just put me through the test and let my actions speak for themselves."

"Listen' at her y'all. Ms. Peaches! I must say, I'm quite enthused at how we've managed to maintain our friendship for so long."

"Simple. Since I've known you you've done nothing but treated me like the queen I am. Can't no woman in the world ask for anything better."

"Thank you for sharing that."

"What about wifey'? What she had to say about all this? You think she strong enough to withstand this type of experience?"

"She seems to be pretty focus but it's only been two weeks. We'll just have to wait and see."

"Like I said, if worst comes to worst with that, I'm here."

"Speaking of relationships, me and you at your shop before I got locked up, what exactly happened?"

"What do you think?"

"A serious mistake was made if you ask me. One that must remain unknown at all cost."

"Have you ever known me to run my mouth about my business? Especially as something as personal as that. To share a lil' secret with you, I got plenty more of where that came from if you decided to be with me."

"Peaches, it's obvious there's still some love I have for you but I'm in too deep with what I have at home. You do understand don't you?"

"Yeah. No problem. I can wait. Patience is a virtue."

"You don't quit do you?"

"Never will."

"By the way, the next time you come see me, don't take so long reaching your destination. It's a jungle in here! A man is subject to not make it out here alive you know," smiled Nard

"You're a big boy. I think you can handle yourself very well."

CHAPTER 27

Shontae spotted sight of her work chair, relieved she made it through a hectic morning. Her day started off awakening an hour late. Asia patiently awaited on the couch. Book bag on her lap. She stumbled out her room in a rush noticing her daughter just sitting there.

"How come you didn't wake mommy up?"

"I didn't want to disturb you. You said to never bother you while you was sleep unless it's an emergency."

She had no time to explain of her daughter error and rushed them both out the door. On her way to meet Ms. Hick and Mike at the lawyers office, she accidentally punched in the wrong address in her navigation system which she ended up on the opposite side of town.

Naomi rolled up beside her chair inside the cubicle.

"Damn you late!"

"I know, right. One of those morning. You wouldn't BELIEVE what I went through. Lets just hope the boss doesn't chew me out about it."

"It's a possibility. But since we're on the topic of our wonderful boss, let me ask you a question, do you find him attractive or VERY attractive?"

"You know I can't answer that. For God's sake, I'm married!"

"I'm not doubting that but between me and you and with me being the great observer that I am-"

"And nosy!"

"That too but from what I've witnessed in this building over the last hour and I could be wrong, though I doubt it, but I honestly believe our boss is strongly attracted to someone in this room."

"You don't think he's mixing business with pleasure do you?"

"Hell, why not? They say over thirty some percent of relationships occurs at the work place and there are a lot of young women around here, including us, who got it going on for themselves."

"So maybe you're his top candidate?"

"Nope! I'm not the one being asked of my whereabouts every minute over the past hour."

"He stalkin' her like that?"

"Is he! I don't know why he hasn't given her her own personal phone so she can check in with him."

"Well, who is she then?"

Naomi twirled around in her chair. Eyes closed. Finger pointed. Shontae watched as her seat came to a stop.

"Who, ME," acknowledging the finger pointed directly at her.

"Yep," nodding in agreement.

"Get out of here! You can't be serious!"

"Listen, now I know your ring symbolized everything but this man has asked me over a thousand times of your whereabouts."

"So he IS trippin' bout' me being so late. Did he sound mad?"

"Not the slightest. In fact, watch this," pressing a button on the phone at Shontae's desk. "Excuse me, Mr. Smith, Mrs. Hick has finally made it in sir. Would you-"

"Yes-yes! Please, send her to my office."

Glancing up at Shontae, "See what I mean."

After her long morning, the last thing she wanted to partake in was a heated argument about her tardiness but had no choice. Her boss had every right to express his opinion if not worse. She looked back at Naomi signaling her to move in the direction of his office. He awaited at his desk. Arms crossed. Smiling. Thrilled by her sight and less concern with her tardiness.

"Please, please," standing to his feet. "have a seat Mrs. Hick." She sat at the front of his desk uncertain of where his friendly greeting was headed. "How are you feeling? Is everything okay?" She nodded cautiously. "Lets get to the point shall we. Good. Okay, the reason why I've been requesting of your presence in my office was because of the bad news I got not long ago about your husband being locked up. Something bout' gun trafficking I believe."

"Sir," raising out her seat, "I appreciate your concern and all but this is none of your business."

She headed for the door. He quickly caught up before she made an exit.

"Yes, yes and I understand all that but my concern has to deal more with the victim wife."

"And what about me."

"Please, have a seat and allow me to finish explaining myself."

"I'll stand," feeling angered at him knowing of her husband incarceration.

"No problem but at least hear me out," taking a seat at his desk. "Now, I clearly understand that it's none of my business but when something this serious involves my worker, my best worker, it's only right that I express my deepest concern and possibly be of some serious help. That is, if I can in some way."

"Mr. Smith-"

"Antonio."

"Antonio, thank you for the offer and everything but I think our lawyer can handle it from here.

He stayed seated watching her depart.

"Mrs. Hick," pausing herself at the door, "I know of the prosecutor building the case against your husband and his friend. We socialize from time to time. He was my classmate in college and we kept in touch ever since. He also owes me a favor and whom better suited for it to be used on other than my number one worker?"

"And what favor do I owe you in return Mr. Antonio? You know they say nothing in life comes free."

"Those are just sayings. What I seek in return is priceless." He shuffled under a stack of papers on his desk retrieving a small card. "Here."

"And what is this," taking hold of it.

"The instructions are on the back and remember, a lifetime event like this," pointing at what she held on to, "is what make dreams a reality."

She studied his eyes and later read the card. A yacht with 'DREAMGIRL' written on it laced the front part and on back were words stating: A LIMO TO ARRIVE AT 5 P.M. A SMALL BOAT TO BRING YOU TO MY YACHT OFF THE COST OF SAVANNAH AT TEN. BY 10:15, A YACHTING ADVENTURE TO MEET THE MORNING SUNSHINE! She looked up at him without speaking a word and slid it in her pocket. Naomi waited for her friend to sit at her desk.

"Well, what did he say?" Shontae stared at her speechless. "Are you gone say something or do I have to shake it out of you?"

Parting her lips, "Are there big sharks in the Atlantic Ocean?"

"Say what?"

"Mommy! Mommy," knocking on her bedroom door.

"Come in Asia."

"Mommy," climbing atop of her bed. "I can't sleep."

"And why is that my little queen?"

"I miss my daddy."

"I miss him too but we have to be strong and stick together until he comes home."

She sat up against the head board. Asia embraced under her arm.

"And when is that mommy?"

"I talked with God tonight before mommy laid down asking him about daddy."

"And what did he say?"

"He said for us not to worry our pretty lil' heads so much. He also said that he'll send daddy to us sooner than we think as long as we continue to one, stay out of trouble. Two, make good grades in school and three, continue saying our prayers every night. You have been saying your prayers haven't you angel face?"

"Yes, mamm. Even at school in the girl bathroom when no one was in there but me I said them alone. I cried after I finished."

"You did?"

"Yeah' mommy. I made a good grade on a test the teacher handed us back and the first thing I thought about was daddy wanting to show him but," lowering her head "he wasn't home."

"Mommy hurt sometimes about daddy not being home too Asia. It's not easy at all for me but like I said earlier, we have to be strong. Can you promise me that?"

"I'll make a deal with you mommy. I promise to be strong if you let me sleep in here with you tonight."

"And who taught you how to bargain like that young lady?"

"My daddy."

"It figured. But under one condition, you sleep on your side of the bed and I'll sleep on mines. Deal?"

"Deal mommy."

She slid underneath the covers.

"Good night Asia and Asia-"

"Mamm."

"Always keep your prayers high to the sky."

"I will mommy. Good night."

She lay awake wondering in what direction her family was headed or was she wrong in pocketing the card handed to her at work. The message had clearly been established to her boss how much she loved her husband and felt no need to fret about the invitation to his yacht. She figured the social gathering with him and a few others would be relieving. Plus, beneficial in finding out more on just how helpful his friend, the prosecutor, could really be with the situation. She needed him home. Her daughter even more. The trip was in a week. Enough time to inform her husband of a better day if all else fails. Nard approving of the help is what concerned her the most but at this stage, he really had no other option if he wanted his freedom. His stay at the county jail seem permanent for now and any help offered would be highly appreciated.

CHAPTER 28

"**O**kay Mr. Hick," placing his briefcase atop of a rusted table engraved with various names of those who were there before him, "lets get down to business shall we. The best thing in your favor at this time is that you have no prior convictions which is a big plus. Secondly, you're charged with accessory to a crime and what that means is that you might've acted in a criminal state of mind with the intent to help but only to a certain extent. Now with a plea, you're looking at thirty-six months including jail time while caged in this-this," looking around at graffiti scribbled on walls in a room slightly larger than a bathroom, "hell-hole. You'll do no more than maybe thirty months. Depend on how long they keep you here. If you go to trail and blow it, five years and do a lil' over four years maybe."

"Maaan, I ain't done jack! Therefore, I ain't pleadin' to nuthin'! What I look like takin' a plea? Like I told them when I first got arrested, I just rode with the man on a business trip. Nuthin' else! He works where I work at. I ain't' pleadin' out. No sir! No way! And that's for sure."

"According to your co-defendant, you WERE the lookout man."

"That's what he said? BULLSHIT! Go' head on with that foolishness man. I was asleep when they tapped on the window. Some lookout man I was."

"If you ask me, my advice to you would be to take the plea."

"If I wanted your advice I would've asked for it but I'm payin' for your legal services and we ARE going to trail. I don't need this bogus conviction on my record."

"Are you sure this is what you want to do Mr. Hick?"

"Go and tell the judge I said to meet me at his bench whenever he's ready."

"Alright sir," stuffing his paperwork back into the briefcase, "have it your way. I'll let them know to choose twelve from hell A.S.A.P."

"You do that and make sure you put on your best suit and tie also."

CHAPTER 29

"**I**t sure feels good to finally be back home. Thank you Jesus! For a minute there I thought the hospital bed had become my permanent place of rest."

"Oh stop sayin' that momma'! Everyone knows you're the biggest fighter on this side of the globe."

"I ain't to sure bout' that. Anymore fightin' with that situation and y'all might've had to count me out. Where's my lady Fur? You seen my baby? Here kitty, kitty, kitty! Lady Fur," placing her belongings down on the floor. She hadn't been inside but a second searching throughout the house for her best friend.

"MOMMA'! I need to talk to you!"

"What is it child," reentering the living room. "All that hootIn' and hollerIn' you doIn' in here. The neighbors gone think you crazy."

"Have a seat momma'."

"For what? I ain't got time right now. Don't you see me lookIn' for Lady Fur? She somewhere in her hiding from me. Lady Fur!"

Slowly, on one knee, she bent down searching under the couch.

"Okay momma'. Now you're goen' to far."

"Are you gonna' help or just continue to stand there watching me?"

"That's what I want to talk with you about."

"Why? Is something wrong," expressing her concern.

"Just please… have a seat." She stared at her daughter before resting

85

herself. "Now, I know how much that cat means to you. She's been around bout as long, if not longer, then your great grand kids.

"Will you get to the point already. You know my life expectancy is gettin' shorter."

"Momma', somehow how Lady Fur slid out the back door on me while I was tending to your garden and unfortunately, I haven't seen her since. Her bowl of food hasn't been touched lately either."

"How long she been gone?"

"Almost a week."

"And exactly when were you goin' to tell me?"

"When the time presented itself which seem like now."

"My, my, my. My baby is somewhere. Alone! Out there in that cold, cold world. I haven't been out the hospital but two minutes and God remain testing my faith. Um, um, um. I know you didn't mean it on purpose sugah'. Now, if you don't mind, I'm goin' to lay down for a while."

CHAPTER 30

"**O**oooweee child! Let me call you back honey! I think they done released Mike Tyson from prison and he just walked his fine ass in my shop," cooling himself off with a hand fan. "Honey, I don't need to know if I can be of some assistance to you but on what part of your body can the assisting begin?"

M-J wanted to puke at what stood behind the counter. The cashier dressed in a pink t-shirt tied in a knot way above the navel. Daisy duke shorts squeezed tighter than spandex on a pair of muscular thighs. A lime-green ribbon wrapped around the neck did little in concealing an atoms apple the size of a quarter bulging out through the cheap polyester material. "What in the hell is that," laughed Johny Blocka'. Neither race nor whatever proclaimed gender mattered with M-J k noticed it but tried not to notice it as long as the disc was sold to the highest bidder. Their list of places to check started to thin itself out. The best offer so far peaked at two-thousand dollars. "Not bad," M-J figured but knew the price was capable of exceeding it by two to three times more.

"Look here mamm, sir, or whoever you are, I got some exclusive shit in my possession here. Fresh off the press."

"What you workin' with then honey," peering across the counter between his legs, "cause judging by what I see from here, I think I can easily take care of that big-boy."

"Hay! It's right here, sir," lifting the DVD up. "In my hand. Not down there."

"Oooooh, you mean that thang?"

"That's right. This THANG has the latest high school sex scene with not one, but TWO of the finest twins one can ever lay their eyes on starring with yours truly, of course."

"Who, YOU! Um! This will be interesting to watch. Come with me in the back big-boy and let me review what you're packin'."

"It's ACTEN' sir and you gone quit with those queer remarks you keep throwing at me on the sly."

"Calm down sexy. Can't a girl enjoy herself with the guests every once in a while?"

"Sure you can but not with this one."

"Come with me gentlemens."

They followed him down the hallway. A collage of naked men were plastered to the walls.

Leaning towards M-J ear, "This fag crazy aint' he?"

M-J couldn't have agreed more but the matter had to be resolved. Just five more minutes in the man presence at the most and they were done.

"Alright handsome, lets see what we're workin' with here." He pointed a remote at the screen. The screen brightened. He inched closer and watched M-J held one in the doggy-style while the other sister clung to his back, kissing him on the neck. "Oh my! Ain't this special. Look at those biceps."

"Look here mutha'-"

"Please," shielding his face from M-J balled up fist, "Please don't hit me baby. You don't have to hurt me. I'm only being what I am but I must say, I'm very impressed with your performance. Now what would you like for me to do with it?"

"It's funny you should ask. I'm looken' to sell it for one helluva' deal."

"Is that so," picking through his teeth with a half-inch finger nail on his pinky.

"What you say Johny Blocka'? Is ten stacks askin' for to much?"

"Only if he's too cheap to spend it and if so, lets bounce."

"You know what big homie, you might be right." He went and ejected his disc. "Sorry to have disturbed you sir. Have a good day."

"Wait, wait! Where ya'll goin'? We haven't even discussed any type of deals yet."

"Let me put it to you like this, I could probably get over several million hits on the internet for this and get rich overnight."

"Ooooo! Mr. Smaaart one! Ok Mr. Handsom. Question? Does the two women know about your wheelin' and dealin' their private lives on the dotted line?"

He faced his partna' who only turned his head in the opposite direction. "Nah."

"Okay then! The truth is out! Now before I offer you my price, are you sure this is what you wanna' do? Going once. Going twice. Going," awaiting a response.

"Yes!"

"Good. Five thousand dollars. Take it or beat it honey. The choice is yours."

CHAPTER 31

"**D**on't you know that crazy lawyer y'all got me wanted me to take a plea even after I clearly explained to him that I had nothing to do with what got me in here in the first place?"

"And what's wrong with that?

"What's wrong with it! Shontae, when you started drinkin' cause you sound like your drunk as hell right now."

"Like you were the night before you got arrested? Don't think I forgot cause I haven't but right now we have more important issues to deal with and you making the right decision is at the top of that list. I need you home baby. WE need you home. Your daughter is asking of your return almost every day? I mean, what you want me to say? What? Continue lying to her?"

"Nah. Not really. Just keep instilling in her how strong her daddy love is for her and I'll do the rest."

"Easier said than done. They locked you up for being at the wrong place and time and on top of that, they won't even give you a bond NOR are they actin' like they plan on freeing you anytime soon. If worse comes to worse, think about your family first and not just yourself."

"Don't I always."

"You do and I thank you for that."

They sat in silence staring at each other. One with freedom and luxury. The other, freedom in the heart with struggles in the mind.

"Oh, baby, I almost forgot. I got some good news to share with you."

She didn't mean for it to come out the way it did but was also ready to face any of his objections towards it. "I know of someone that could possibly help our situation."

"And what? I suppose that just fell out of the sky and into your lap. And how did you go about gettin' that Mrs. Hick?"

"Lets just say I pulled a few strings."

"That's one helluva' string you pullin' on. And I'm sure a price came with it too."

It did and she promised not to tell a soul.

"Nard, baby, does it even mater?"

"Hell yeah' it matters! Now who assisted you with the favor," becoming hostile.

"My boss."

"Excuse me? I can't hear you. Speak up."

"MY BOSS," screaming through the phone.

"Well, you go back and tell yo' boss thanks, but no thanks."

"DAMIT' NARD! Will you stop being stubborn for once in your life and just think about takin' the damn offer."

"Shontae," moving closer towards the 3'inch fiberglass that separated them, "I'm gone tell you like I told the lawyer earlier this week, make sure to look your prettiest in the court room cause I'll be dressed to kill."

He slammed the phone down and stormed out the room. She sat outside in the parking lot frustrated with his actions. Maybe if she consulted more with Ms. Hick about it that they could come up with a solution to convince Nard not to go trial. A this late in the game, she had no other options.

"Hello, Ms. Hick?"

"Who is this, Shontae?"

"Yes mamm. I tried talking with your son a few minutes ago and he just doesn't seem to listen. He said he's goin' to trial."

"TO TRIAL! Child, tell me you lyin'."

"I wish. What if he's found guilty? What am I supposed to do then? He could get five years. That's a long time! I mean, we got money in the bank but I don't know how long it will last. He also has a daughter AND a son to think about as well."

"Shontae, calm down. Things gonna' be aiight'. My son crazy but he ain't that crazy to. He just playen' the stall game with them. Probably tryen' to see will they gone and throw his charges out."

"But what if they don't? What then?"

"Well, it's like this, pray to the God up above cause' we gone need all of his blessings immediately if they find the poor child of mines guilty."

CHAPTER 32

"**K**anisha'," bursting through the front door of their home, "Kanisha! Where you at girl! Come in the living room!"

She hadn't to long ago dozed off.

"What is it girl, what. This better be important," sliding her feet into a pair of house shoes.

'Kanisha! Hurry up!"

Wiping her face, "Whaaat?"

"Guess what?"

"I know you ain't wake me up to play some guessing game with you?"

"No! I was at work realizing that I had to buy me some pads for … you know what for but anyway, the thought hit me. Hard! So after I did the math and noticed my normal schedule was slightly off, I became suspicious real quick. Then, I decided to test myself for a reassurance and THAT'S when it shocked the hell out of me. And fast!"

"Kandi, I hardly understood a single word you just said. Speak English girl."

"I'm pregnant!

Kanisha felt numb by the words ringing inside her ears.

"You can't be serious?

She reached inside the purse and handed her the pregnancy test.

"Unless these things are inaccurate, you just became an auntie, auntie."

"But how?"

"You won't believe me."

"Try me."

"Remember our small encounter with M-J?"

"Oh … my… God," placing a hand over her mouth. She ran through the house to review her personal calendar. The monthly scheduled displayed a slight discrepancy. "This can't be right," recounting the dates on her fingers. "KANDI!"

Entering her bedroom, "Not you too! What are we gonna' do?"

"Whatever it is, we better do it fast."

"You're not thinking about abortion are you?"

"And why not?"

"Kanisha! How dare you! The last thing on my mind is killing my baby. No way! I'm keepin' it. Him. Her. Whatever the baby is."

"I'm gonna' kill that fool'."

"Will you stop thinken' like that!"

"I'm speakin' of the person responsible for all of this. Does not that mean anything to you? We got one year of school left before college. How we gonna' be able to do both?"

"I'm sure they have some kind of day care on campus."

"And what about us having the same baby-daddy? How that's gonna' look on social media? People gone think we're some kind of crazy freaks. I can't do it Kandi. I just can't."

"Who cares what people think? We have to be responsible for our own actions. So what if we laid down with this one guy who got us both pregnant. BIG DEAL! But I'm not having no abortion. No way in the world am I going through that. You do what you wanna' but my mind is already made up."

Kanisha wanted her sister to be more aware of the damage could have on making the wrong choice for her future. Two kids by the same father was unimaginable for Kandi to phathom. She knew of no one in a similar predicament that she could go and consult with. Maybe when she awoke in the morning it would all be just a bad dream and just laugh it off or if not, check herself into the mental institution. She started to feel woozy from all the horrible thoughts racing through her mind. Kandi sat on the bed without a single doubt about what she wanted to do.

"Here's the deal Kanisha, this is a very serious situation we're facing. I don't know about you but I need some serious time to think on it but first thing in the morning, we're going to the hospital for a definite yea or nay on this subject. You got that?"

"I hear you but it still doesn't change a thing with me. So you do what you gotta' do and I'm gonna' do me. Now if you don't mind, I need to go and check out a few baby items at the mall. Be back shortly."

CHAPTER 33

"**W**hat I don't understand celly is why you wanna' go to trial? You do know who up against don't you? I mean, you have read what that paper of yours said haven't you? Look at your charge and tell me what it says at the top of it." Nard grabbed some papers underneath his mattress. "While you doing that, please allow me the honors on informing you also: UNITED STATES OF AMERICAN versus one lil' fella' …. YOU! Do me a favor bra', I want you to think about this decision you about to make very carefully before you regret it. These people have a ninety-seven to a ninety-eight percent conviction rate. You can't beat them! Look at it this way, it's not the end of the world even if you do plead guilty. Take it as a learning experience. Shit happens! Not just to you but every single soul alive."

"J-Dub, I appreciate yo' jailhouse wisdom and all but this is something that I have to do. True enough they got a big gun pointed directly at my head but fortunately for me, I got a bigger heart."

"With a bigger bulls-eye mark written across it too and on top of that, you said it yourself that yo' wife was gone try and pull a few strings for you. At least think about yo' family. It's not just about you anymore playboy. Runnen' up behind Peaches aint' gone work no more. Oh yeah! I heard bout you. D-Man ol' lady got you caught up in the past with her fine ass. She still sexy aint' she?

"Aint' lost a ounce."

"Damn, damn, damn! The whole city was talken' bout' that shit when it happened. How you pulled that off man? That boy was rich as hell. Yo' local ass just came through and snatched up his ol' lady like it wasn't nuthin'. D-Man was crazy as hell about that one."

"You learn one thing in life and that is…' what's yours today can quickly become someone elses tomorrow."

"Now that's real talk playa'."

"Which is one of the main reason I'm going all the way to trial with this one. We, as black people, we can't keep allowing our oppressor to push us back into one of these shoe boxes they got us sleeping in without a fight. I gotta' show my family that without standing up for something you believe in like your respect, they'll continue kickin' us down to the ground. Treaten' us as if we're animals. No sir! Not me. It ain't in my blood cuss'. From the cradle to the grave is an everyday process of living that must mean something to us. You. Me. Any African American. All I ask is that you give me the support a brotha' gone need."

"Oh, you definitely got that playa. I hear the real shit you kickin'. Kind of remind me of my ol' partna' I used to run with in the streets. He used to always tell me, A man must have some type of G code to live by or else taste sweet bitterness until you die."

"Don't think for a minute that I'm not concern with who my actions gonna' impact but in the end, if everyone plays their part right, we should come out on top for winning the fight. Always believe in you know matter what."

"Man, you should write a book with all that game you spittin'."

"Who knows. Maybe that's out there somewhere in that great big world of ours lined up for a brotha' but first I gotta' clear out a few hurdles in my life and possibly in the end when my mind is more settled, I just might just take that up as a hobby. Who knows."

Nard stretched out on the bunk wondering if Shontae would support his decision in the end regardless of how much she disapproved it. He never meant to walk out on her earlier during visit but the message had been clearly established that he was going to trial with or without her. Being stubborn had nothing to do with his choice of actions this time but more so with the UNITED STATES OF AMERICA, INC. He heard of prisons becoming a big investment for private companies and wanted no parts of its billion doller industry. By pleading guilty meant he committed an act of wrong doing he had no knowledge of. He couldn't sit back and allow his innocence to be swept under the rug. If the color of skin was how the corporate America viewed him then a jail cell is how he'll defend himself through the end.

"Momma, daddy not coming back around no mo' is he?"

"It's more. Not mo'. And what makes you say that?"

"Because …. he just isn't."

"Is that the only answer you have?"

"Yes mamm. Until I can think of something else."

"To answer your question, yes, daddy will be coming back around. We just have to be patient."

"I don't like being patient. I get bored."

"Everybody struggles with patience but when that happens, bad things can happen too."

"Like what momma'?

"For one, lets say you was standing on a street corner trying to cross a road and a car was about to pass. Would you be patient and wait for the car to pass completely or would you try running out in front of the car for NOT being patient?"

"You said to always let the car pass you by first and then cross the street afterwards. That will keep me from getting hit."

"And hurt. And you are exactly right sir. The same thing applys with daddy. If you are not patient enough for daddy's return you will worry your lil' mind crazy. You don't want to go crazy do you?

"No mam."

"Good. So you must be strong like your daddy and continue being the smart lil' child that you are and before you know it, daddy will be home in a blink of an eye."

"No he aint'!"

"Isn't sir. Isn't. And maybe not as fast as we would like him to but trust me son, he will. Now, isn't it beddy-bye?"

"Yes mamm," sounding sullen.

"Come and give mommy a great big kiss my lil' hero." It did little to change his mood and she knew it. "Thank you sir. Now have a good night. Don't forget to shut the door behind you."

"See you in the morning momma."

CHAPTER 34

"**T**hank you for finally comin' aboard Mr. Spock."

"Sure thing Captain. I had to sneak out the church from the family. And plus, who you know wanna' see they partna' stuck off behind an unbreakable glass anyway. You know how it is homeboy."

"Not really. But I'm learning."

"Now you know if the shoe was on the other foot and business was being tookin' care of out there in them streets for me, I wouldn't care if you visit me every leap year when it comes around."

"You say that shit now big-man."

"Only cause' I mean what I say."

"So I guess your main purpose in this here visit today is to try and convince me into not going to trial also?"

"What you think? Though I can't quite understand the reason behind your actions. All I want to know is, why you aint' think about consulting with your right-hand man first. What was so hard about that?"

"Not a thing."

"I can't tell! You probably like several months away from possibly losing not only your trial but everything else you ever worked for. Your career. House. Maybe even your family. What are they suppose to do while you're in here playin' the righteous brotha'? Do you really think that P.Y.T. of yours at home gonna' actually wait on you?"

"I don't see why not. Our marriage means more than just a ring."

"Is that so?"

"You damn right!"

"We homeboys right?"

"Tighter than a nats' ass."

"So that means you can handle the truth then right?"

"Take your best shot."

"Between me and you, I think this might be the DUMBEST ass mistake you'll ever make in your life."

"And what makes you so sure about that?"

"Cause it's obvious! You're only concern with yourself right now. Not your kids. Your wife. And what about your grandmother? I bet you haven't even given that any serious thought have you? There's no way in hell you could have. Not a major decision like this one. Impossible!"

Mike had no urgency in visiting his friend while caged up like a slave. Shenequa informed him of the mistake Nard was about to make and decided to pay him a visit before it was too late.

"What you think I should do Mike? Go 'head. Tell me. You think I should just stand there before the judge, spill my guts out about something I have no knowledge of and ask them to walk me off to my temporary place of stay until I'm released? Is that the way a real man goes about handling things?"

"We both know the answer to that but sometimes a real man has to compromise on certain scenarios and this being one of them. We don't need you in cell block seven but out here in society. Sooner than later."

He agreed with him one hundred percent. Sometimes one must put aside selfish motives and be considerate of others. Especially when involving family. But it still didn't change the fact he was innocent and the only reasonable route to prevail would be by going to trial.

"As much as I want to my friend…. I can't. I just can't. I'm sorry."

"You know your mother gone kill me right? She told me if I'm not successful with you to just gone and find me a place in here for the duration."

"That's my momma'. Always demanding stuff."

"And her son. Always being hard-headed."

"Thank you for payin' your partna' a visit"

"You betta' preciate' it cause it'll be a while before I come back to this ratchet place."

"How my nephew doin'? Still on the run?"

"Not any more. She finally allowed him back in. The tension with them is slightly lingering in the air still but it'll eventually simmer down."

"That's good to know. Break up to make up."

"You straight in here, right?'

"A lil' bit. Just learning more on how to adapt. Everything is issued to you in here. Soap. Deodorant. Face rags and towels. Dingy ass jump suits. No socks. They got us walkin' around in shower shoes all day. Feet sweatin' like hell."

"Don't worry about your son either. I'll check up on him on the regular."

"Preciate' that Mike."

"Nard, dawg', we love you out here man and whatever choice you make, you got my full support."

"You're a good man Mike. It's easy to see why our friendship still endure till this day. Blood brothas' to the end.

"Blood brothas' til' the end! Well my friend, I guess I'll be seing you in the future and remember one thing...guard your grill cause' the jungle will kill."

"Most definitely."

CHAPTER 35

"That was good lookin' out on y'all lettin' a brotha' rest his head there for a while. You think the couple hundred I gave your mother was enough?"

"Fa'sho! We spent that just fine."

"Just don't forget about your long-tale friends out in the basement. Mozarrella is their favorite choice."

"Now that you're gone, they can get all they want and some."

Kanisha barged her way between their space and pent Nard against his locker. Johny Blocka' attempted at confronting her but was stopped by Kandi. Her eyes warned him of any sudden move and there would be serious repercussion.

"WOMAN," blurted M-J. "Are you crazy!"

"Shut up! Just shut up! I ought to kick you in your you know what!"

"Go 'head girl," sided Kandi. "I got your back!"

"Kanisha," spoke Johny Blocka', "will you call this pitbull off me?"

"Johny Blocka', you can take a walk," informed Kanisha. "M-J will get with you later."

"Woman, be fo'real!" The twins doubled up in front of him in awaitance of his departure. "M-J, homeboy, I got your back ...waaaaay back down this hallway somewhere. Just yell for me if it gets too out of hand for you."

"What's this all about," asked M-J.

"M-J, I got something very important to inform you on. In fact, WE" pointing at her and Kandi, "have something important to tell you."

"Can it wait? We're late for class. School work before bed work you know," showing all his teeth. Kandi swung an open palm at his face dodging it by an inch. "Try that shit again woman! Go 'head! Try it!"

"Both you two stop it!" She waited for their hostility to subside stating, "I got one question for you M-J. Just one...simple...question."

"Speak. I'm listenin'."

"How ... HOW did you do it?"

"Do what? Girl, what you talkin' bout'?"

"You heard her," punching his side. "How did you do it?"

"Do what," clutching his lower rib in slight pain. "Can we find somewhere else that's private to talk. I don't want nobody see me drop yo' sister." They relocated inside the girls bathroom. Kandi stood guard next to the door disallowing anyone from entering. "Now, would somebody mind fillin' me in on what's goin' on?"

"You must first promise me, on your unborn kids, not to tell a single soul of what I'm about to share with you?"

"Unborn kids? HA! Aint' that a funny one. But anyway, you got my word."

"Michael Turner Junior ... you are soon to be the proud father of," looking back at Kandi, "I can't say it."

"We're both pregnant by you M-J. There! See how easy that way sis'."

"Why y'all playin'? All this commotion for a measly joke? Well, ha, ha, ha. Now let me get the hell up out of here."

"Not so fast," blocking his path at the door. "You got some serious explaining to do."

"M-J, she's right. We're both pregnant but what I can't understand is how."

"I should be askin' y'all the same thing. Nobody was on the pill or anything? I thought about using protection but hell, we had got so caught up in the moment that any precautions to take just went out the window. But damn! You said BOTH of ya'll pregnant? I mean by the grace of God I tried avoiding my room by all means but you two insisted on seeing what it looked like inside my house and before I knew anything, we was all seeing what each of us look like without any clothes on."

"BULLSHIT," shouted Kandi. "Bullshit, bullshit, bullshit!"

"No, real shit. Now, it's gottin' even realer."

"Kanisha requested of being a murderer. I bid to differ."

"Kanisha isn't either. Ain't that right Kanisha?"

"You two are crazy! Are y'all even aware of what we've done?"

"Looks to me like we've started one big happy family...momma'," joshed M-J.

It appeared she had no win. Kanisha dug off in her pocket and retrieved the test result written on a medical slip supporting her facts. Two women of identical features were pregnant by one man.

M-J slumped down at a desk in back of the class. Startled. Dreams of a successful future shattering right before his eyes. Everything depended on him gaining a scholarship which now seem improbable. He barely had a place to call home. His mother ultimatum was clear and simple: "Graduation ... AND OUT MY HOUSE!" Without a steady source of income, everything seem dim. Troublesome. "THE DVD!" The crowded room was taken aback by his outburst. He jumped up running out the classroom.

"MR. TURNER! MR. TURNER," yelled the teacher. "WHERE ARE YOU GOING? CLASS ISN'T OVER!"

He raced through the hallway in search of Johny Blocka', finding him asleep inside the gym.

"Big fella'? Big fella'," shaking him awake, "we got trouble. Big trouble!"

Eyelids partially parting, "When a man is resting, what does that mean?"

"Say what! Man, you talken' in yo' sleep. Wake yo' ass up!"

"You gone be layln' in yo' sleep when I finish two-piecin' you to the ground."

"Get serious big fella'. You gotta' ride with me back to the porn shop."

"I thought that deal had already been finalized?"

"It was. That is, before what was in the dark came to light."

"Update me playa'."

"I certainly will big-homie'. I certainly will," patting him on the back. "Come on. Lets get out of here."

CHAPTER 36

"You finally decided to let the poor child back home. I'm very proud of you Shenequa. You're not such a butt-head after all."

"I must be something. Especially after so many years of being friends with Geicos big sister."

"Not today baby girl. Not today. Bills need paid and I aint' found me a man to lay with yet. This shit is becomin' a problem."

"Quit runnin' them all off then."

"If only you knew why. Every time I put this candy on they tongue, they always come up for air talkin' that crazy talk. Wantin' me to marry them."

"What's wrong with that?

"I aint' you like you aint' me. Different strokes for different folks. I like the pleasure of using a man more so than being his personal whore."

"I aint' no whore!"

"Did I say you were? Quit being so defensive. Let your guards down some. I'm referring to those who live on they hands and knees just for the doggy bone. The whole world know you run your house-hold."

"And make sure you get that clearly understood too sistah' gal!"

"So what's the latest on Nard? He getten' out soon?"

"Fat chance! Everything looks to be an uphill battle from here."

"Does the boy know what he's doin'?"

"By goin' to trial? Not at all child. His pride is definitely in the way."

"Fo'real! Don't he know what them people are capable of doing to him?

The fed's sent my cousin to prison for thirty years behind a hundred dollas' worth of crack. Thirty years! Can you believe that? That's preposterous."

"And crazy."

"He playin' with them folks aint' he? Please tell me he aint' serious and if he is, somebody needs to hurry up and get down there to convince him otherwise before they put him into hibernation for the rest of his life."

"Mike done tried all of that. Even his wife. Nothing seems to work. I've learned one thing about a man and his pride. When it comes time to thinkin' rationale, both his lil' brain AND his lil' thang end up on the shorter end of the stick."

"Now that is so true. For once Tosha, you have really impressed me with your mind. I'm glad to see I have started to rub off on you in the right way."

"Yeah. I guess you're right but have we forgotten, it was I who chose you as a friend for your brawn. Not brain. Now get to thinkin' on a exit plan out of here. Come on! Scat! You know the routine," lifting Shenequa up off the couch.

"One of these days Tosha I'm gonna' toss you so far out my house that you'll never be able to make it back to this place we call life. A woman lost at land, ocean and sea somewhere beyond our galaxy."

Stationed at her front door, "You always have look better going than comin' but how you manage to talk out the back of your head like that remains a mystery yet to be unsolved. Have a good, I mean, a terrible day."

CHAPTER 37

"Can you imagine what everyone gone think of you now? Do you realize how much this is gonna' make your name stand out over anything else? Not only did you bag two women of the exact same features but you got them BOTH pregnant. You might can get away with them being on the DVD but you can't hide this one. No way in hell."

"Which is why we're headed back to the porno shop. It's a must we get that back."

"Oooooooo-snap? Daaaaamn! I almost forgot. You sold it! And even spent over half the money. That's crazy! You got two baby mothers, in the porno bizz', who are about to have your babies. Tell me, how does that feel?"

"The same way with someone pullin' they foot out yo' ass."

"It is sort of big and soft back there aint' it. You see it! Go 'head. Touch it," lifting part of his huge butt off the seat. He grabbed M-J's wrist forcing his hand to touch it.

"Not at this moment homey'," pulling it loose. "We got more important things to attend to right now."

"What I want to know is where you gone come up with the other half of what you already done spent."

"I'll figure something out once we get there but there's a great lesson to be learnt here."

"Which is?"

"Shit only piles as high as one sit."

"I guess the statue of liberty must be wipin' her face clean of plenty shit right now cause yo' ass is sittin' high on that crown."

The homosexual paused at the sight of them walking inside. He rushed from behind the counter.

"Oh my gooooooooooooodness! Look who's back," arms spreaded wide running up to M-J.

"Watch it sucka;" shoving the man away from him. "I done told you once bout' playin' child games with a grown man.

"Did ya'll miss Miss Pinky? Couldn't stop thinken' bout the kitty I suppose?

She's here! And purring louder than ever."

"Look here man, the only reason I'm back is because you got something very important I need."

"Now that, I do. Where do you want it at? Out here? In front of your friend? At least let me lock the door first."

M-J yank hold of his arm pulling him closer.

"Look here bitch! Stop it! You here me. Stop it! All I want is the DVD back from you. That's it. The DVD and I promise you you'll never see me again."

"Would you mind lettin' this sensitive arm of mines go? You're hurtin' her sir."

M-J pushed him back. "That won't be a problem. Just hand over the $5,000's.

Eyeing his friend, "We got half of it right now. I'll pay you the rest in a week or two."

"Oh no honey. No cash, no goin' to the stash."

"Look here, you don't understand. It's very important I get that back."

"Hellooooooooooo," snapping his finger in the air, "are you listenin' to me honey'? Let me repeat this a lil' bit slower. No... cash... no ... stash."

"No stash you say," quickly squeezing hold of him around the upper arms. "You gone give me that DVD or find yo' self sweepIn' this floor off with your face."

"Aiight' M-J. Take it easy home boy. I'm sure Miss. Pinky gone do the right thing. Aren't we Miss. Pinky?"

"Ye-yesss," enduring the pain from his harden squeeze. He turned him loose.

"As soon as you give me the full amount. Other than that, I'm sorry. You can beat me up. Break me in half. I don't care but the DVD stays until the bill is fully paid."

"Aiight', aiight', aiight'. Let's be reasonable here. There is one way I might can come up with the rest of the money."

"You don't say? Well, I'll have a seat right over there honey cause' I am all ears."

CHAPTER 38

The weight of her body felt light. Head slightly nauseated. She held on to the rail as the boat sailed through unsettled water. Antonio and several of his friends were below deck. Their company had started to bore her senseless with small talk of celebrity gossip. A breath of fresh air seemed the best remedy to a dull night and excused herself.

No one back home knew of her brief getaway. Her daughter was left in the care of her grandmother. The plan was to return before noon without having been missed. With all that was happening in her life, she decided the time away would do her some good.

Everything went according to plan as written on back of the card. Most of her time during the four-hour ride was spent questioning if she had made the right or wrong choice: Right for deserving a break from reality; Wrong for disobeying her husband. She decided it was too late to turn back now and stretched out in her seat.

"Are we enjoying ourselves yet," disturbing her peace.

"Besides your corny friends, everything else has been quite fascinating. Oh, and the swaying of this boat is one to get familiar with too."

"The water is a lil' bit edgy tonight. Hopefully she'll settle more as the night continues."

"I really appreciate your invitation. Give me some time to clear my mind on a few things."

"Mainly your husband."

"He refused any of your assistance. Why, I don't know. He's being very stubborn for some reason. It's like he has a chip on his shoulder. There's no doubt in my mind my husband is innocent but you, along with the rest of the world, know the government doesn't play fair with anyone."

"Are they plan on releasing him anytime soon?"

"Judging by what the lawyer said, I seriously doubt it. He wants him to take a plea of thirty-six months."

"With a few education programs they offer behind bars, that should reduce his sentence even more."

"My husband thinks goin' to trial will prove a manly point or something he was trying to explain to me. I can't remember."

"Hay, what can I say. Men will be men. Always trying to convince themselves they're the toughest while overlooking who they'll hurt in the process."

"It's called ego-ignorish."

"That's a good way of putting it."

"But that only leaves me stranded with our daughter and other important business to deal with by myself."

"Well, not quite."

"And how so?"

"All the assistance you'll need is standing just a few inches away from you."

"Please don't get it confuse Mr. Smith. I only came on this trip because of all the hard work I've put into back at the firm. I felt I deserve this."

"So what you're tellin' me is that I've been used?"

"I guess you can say that but in a harmless way. You said it yourself that I'm your number one worker."

"And you're also my number one choice for spending a cozy moment alone with as well."

It happened again! His hand gripped tight around her wrist. The first time it happened in his office she managed an escape to her cubicle. A second time proved more than just a coincidence. Except for this time, her chance at escaping seem inevitable.

"Trust me Shontae. I respect your happily-ever-after-marriage one hundred percent but that look, that-that glare. It's something in your eyes. Something more pleasing than a dream. More imaginable than a fantasy." He freed her wrist. "Greater than any blessing and as I stand here, in front of you, it's only right of me to take advantage of your presence and not a disadvantage of your generosity. What I'm really tryin' to say to you Mrs. Hick is-"

"There you two are! HAY GUYS! I FOUND THEM! THEIR OUT HERE ON THE TOP DECK," interrupted Cindy. Shontae felt relieved their privacy had been interrupted. "We were just about to start playen' Scrabble without you two guys,"

"Give me a few minutes would you Cindy?"

"Aiight' you two love-birds but once we start, ya'll might have to wait for another hour before the next one begin. I hate stopping in the middle of one just to start another," she mentioned while departing back down the stairs.

"Now, if you don't mind me reconvening, where was I?

"Explaining how God blessed you with the greatest gift ever."

"And how'd you guess?"

"Because it just dove overboard."

"SHONTAE! SHONTAE! WHAT ARE YOU DO'EN! WAIT! COME BACK!"

CHAPTER 39

Nard somehow managed to view through the narrow window in the wall while standing from atop of his bunk. A thin coat of winter snow blanketed some of the yards and homes overnight. The night clouds no longer linger overhead, only the early sign of dawn. A pocket radio informed them that evening of a possible snow storm occurring around nightfall. Shortly before midnight, he dozed off missing out on the first snowflake falling to the ground. A hand was placed against the slender window unsure if the cold he felt was because of the outside chill or from the freezing cell.

He climbed down off the bunk trying not to disturb his cellmate slumber. A rag doused in warm water and squeezed dry at the sink was used to wash his face with. The short handle toothbrush complicated matters with keeping a closed mouth while brushing his teeth. Commissary sold only snacks and medication forcing the usage of other hygienic supplies issued at the Muscogee county jail.

"For a first time offender," lifting his head from underneath the covers, "you sure as hell know how to move in silence."

Looking back at him through the mirror, "Thanks. I practice what I expect out of the next man to practice which is respect."

"Well," shifting his body towards the wall, "you definitely got my vote on that one."

He attempted a late response but heard light sounds of snoring. Certain adjustment to life inside prison wasn't as complicated as one described to him in the past. Minding his business, a trait instilled in him by both parents, lessen his chances of any unnecessary trouble. It didn't take long before he witnessed an acquaintance in the dorm experience a gruesome beaten for trying to steal another man breakfast meal. J-Dub stressed the importance of resting with one eyelid open and the other close unknowing what enemy possibly lurk amongst their unit.

Other survival habits he adapted to over a period of time prepared him for what might be a longer vacation than expected after today. His trial was at 9 A.M. Time he neither dwelt on nor worried himself with. Shontae accused him of making the decision to go to trial out of spite, an answer he struggled to cope with. His immediate family was furiated in the beginning but sided with his final decision. Miss Hick shared with her son of challenging his true strength came only in the form of knowing your true self and by facing the government without a weary bone in his body meant a future gain of prosperity.

Several inmates walked around wrapped in blankets thrown over their head and shoulders fending off the cold day room. He noticed no one in the area where he performed his routine push-ups and hurried to its location.

"You Nard aint'cha?"

Raising to his feet, "Yeah. That's me. How can I assist you?"

"Didn't mean to bother you this early sir."

"You aiight'. But what's up?"

Judging by his appearance, Nard figured the man to be a rehabilitated crackhead or at least until released back into the streets to commit another petty offense for his habit which more than likely landed him there in the first place.

"I came in here last night from another unit. Someone had dropped a kite on me about being the thief of the block."

"Lets hope THAT'S not true."

"Man, look here. I've done a lot of things in my lifetime but stealin' aint' one of them."

"No offense sir but I'm sort of busy right now."

"Aiight', aiight'. Check this out. Yo' co-defendant-"

"How you know my co-defendant" disallowing a finish in his statement. "In fact how you know me?"

"He described you to me. He was in the dorm I came from. Anyway, he said for you to take a plea. Something bout' not makin' it harder on yourself."

"Is that so. Is that all he said," reconvening with his exercise.

"I believe so but, you wouldn't have something I can eat? I'm starvin' man."

Standing to his feet, "I got a lil' something that'll hold you down till breakfast but first, answer this simple question for me."

"What is it?"

"Does he think for one minute that I'm him?"

"I'm not understanding you."

"Good. Cause what you so-call stated he said, he aint' feelin' it either."

The message forced an extended workout beyond his usual forty minutes. His co-defendant message was not quite what he wanted to hear. "Do the right thing he says! Man, this fool crazy," storming inside his cell.

'WHAT! WHAT," springing up off the cot with both his fist balled up. "Who that want they ass kick! Bring it on chump! Bring it on!"

"My bad J."

"Maaaan'," laying back down, "I thought someone was lookin' for some trouble as loud as that door slam. You probably woke the entire dorm with that one."

"You won't believe what just happened."

"Tell me later. Nicki Minaj wants me to bring another shawty' to our personal gathering."

"Some dude that came in here last night had a message for me."

"Must've been pretty shitty' as much force you used in closing that door."

"This fool done sent word talkin' bout' do the right thing and take a plea. Can you believe this dude!"

"Look here homeboy, calm yo'self down and save some of that energy for the courts this mornin'. You got a big day ahead of you. So gone and get you a lil' more rest before they call your name."

"As bad as I want to, I can't. That bullshit got me steamed right now. I'm in this mess because of his ass and he tells me to do the right thing."

"Try not to worry yo'self crazy about it. The truth will prevail. Always live knowing that. Now, if you don't mind, I'll holla' back later."

The furthest thing on his mind was lying down on what felt like the actual ground. A steaming shower seem the better solution in settling his nerves. He grabbed hold of several items and headed to the double shower stalls shared by a population of eighty inmates. The splashing water to his face eased the frustration a tad bit. He couldn't help contemplating on why someone would allow another man to get caught up in something they had no actual knowledge of. Maybe the truth wouldn't prevail at trial. He quickly erased the thought out his mind convinced that his freedom was only a few hours away regardless if anyone helped him or not.

"Mike, Mike? Get yo' butt up boy! We're runnin' late for Nard's trial."

"Do we have to," hugging his pillow tighter. "Everybody know the kangaroo courtroom is gonna' railroad my dawg' without any Vaseline. I just hate the fact that I gotta' go and be a witness to this massacre."

"You aint' lyin' bout that but we still gotta' hurry up and get dress. I'm not tryin' to miss out on any of the foolishness they might try to get away with him. He needs our support."

"You got my clothes already iron for me don't you?

"Negro please! You mean to tell me you didn't do it last night?"

"Woman, we was too busy makin' out remember."

"Is that what you call that? HA! I could've gotten' more excitement out of watching a Mike Tyson classic when he was in his prime knocking them out faster than sixty seconds."

"Miss. Joke-a-lishess you say they call you."

"Miss. Kickin' assess if you don't get you butt up. Hurry up Mike!"

CHAPTER 40

"**I**s this yo' main reason for hitchin' a ride with me? All so you can worry me silly? It's been a long time since I put someone out on side of the road but you headed in the right direction. Keep it up."

"For your information … MISS HICK, I figured we could get along long enough to make it to our son trial without us disputing so much on our past differences and by the way, thank you for the ride."

"Yeah, right. I'm sure you would say that seeing that the power is in my hands now but you aiight'… for now. But I'm sure you'll screw it up. You always have and me knowing you, you always will."

"Lets just hope that's not the case for our son. Do you think he's facin' hard times? I mean', seriously, do you honestly believe for one minute the boy stands a god-given chance in hell against the most crooked system in the world? If you wanna' know the truth, I'd say all the odds are stacked against him. Maybe on a future appeal he'll possibly prevail but at trial? Today? In a federal courtroom? Not…a…chance…"

"Litsin at'cha! We talkin' bout' the future of our second child and here you are sounding more foolish than our former president George Bush junior actin' like he's really concern about the poor and unfortunate in America."

"He said something about my poverty condition? When?"

"You still a lil' slow aint' you but I'm gone work with you. Don't even trip. Anyway, see, the only people that man really cared about is them tycoons ridin' horseback on that billion dolla' oil ranch of his. With him, if it aint' the wealthy, he don't give a damn about the unwealthy."

"Now that, young lady, might be sad but a true statement."

"You ever see him donate anything to someone besides the middle finger on T.V.? Just look behind that evil grin and those two devilish ears pointing straight up on side of his head. All he sayin' is, 'I got ya'll ass now'! Oh yeah. He means business."

"Scandalous game these people play with our race."

"Not when we're the one makin' it easy for them. We the one who handed the struggle of torch back over to them talkin' bout we tired. We give up. We just can't fully blame the devil for what happened to us. Most of us got lost in the sauce by actin' like we got a pale complexion or something. Oh Mr. Willie Lynch went to lettin' some of us party on that pretty front lawn of his while drinkin that good ol' champagne and wine and by nightfall, we fell asleep in an area that looked nothing like our own. But came the next mornen' and that's when all hell broke loose. Mad at the unwashed dishes in the sink at home. Clothes thrown everywhere. Another life-like rerun of "What's Happening" for the million time that goes on and on."

"So we ended' up hatin' more of what we saw at home and who we were?"

"Exactly. Love is the true motivation that we possess behind any real survival or struggle. Without it, you have nothing. Like our son today. Even if he does lose, he'll be aiight'. That boy was born with plenty of love. Where he gets it from beats the hell out of me cause you and I both know that my hate can run deep towards a no-good filthy creep. No offense sir."

"Talk wreckless all you want miss. I'm just enjoyin' the ride."

"However this turmoil turns out, he got my back to the very end."

"Don't leave me out of it. I played a major part of his existence as much as you did and aint' no way in the world I'll leave him stranded by himself like that. Not when he need us the most."

"You know, the more you talk the more I'm startin' to like you."

"So does that mean a second chance?"

"Watch it sucka'! Just one press of this here button on my door and all we'll hear out of you is Geronimooooooo. Straight out that door. Nose first."

"How bout I recline back and silence myself long enough until we reach our destiny."

"Gráciás you ol' fool."

CHAPTER 41

"You and that bus pass of yours been commutin' pretty regularly here lately for quite some time now. My question to you homeboy is how well do you think that's gonna' holdup in a couple more months with twins snuggled up tight in both your arms?"

"Good question."

"What's up with a good answer then? You do have one don't you?"

"Not at this moment but I'm definitely workin' on one. Or two. Maybe three. You got any options available?"

"How bout' this one... J.O.B.! Every parent needs one and yo' butt still lacks any steady income. Football season is over. No more excuses dawg'."

"How ol' you say you were Blocka'?"

"What that got to do with anything? But since you wanna' be so smart about it lets just say ol' enough to fold and mold you into a better man than what you already are."

"Aint' you same the one who struggled with unfolding a triple decker beef and cheese sandwich out its wrapper?"

"How was I to know they had stapled it together holden' that big boy in place."

"I still got my hairy friend hear," patting him on the shoulder, "to help out with transportation every once in a while."

"Which reminds me dawg', M-J, I got a chickenhead' that I can go and layup in now meaning your free rides are gonna' be cut back to a minimum."

"You got a WHAT? Get out of here! Not ol' Johny Blocka' the giant? When did this happen? What, about a century ago" laughed M-J.

"I see everything is funny to you but lets see how long that smile of yours is gone last with your babies off to the side in their carriages laughin' at you for tryin' to hitch ya'll a ride."

"It's just hard to believe big homie."

"Well, believe it. In fact, as soon as I drop you off at your uncle trial, we bout' to hook up and do the, umm, you know what time it is."

"I thought you was comin' inside for a while to get a glimpse at the incorporated system."

"No need. Anytime they lock one of us up, some white man pocket gets fatter and anytime we sit out in the crowd of a courtroom, some white man is observing us for a potential prospect for a possible profit. I'm sure you'll fill me in on it later. Pracilla needs her big daddy."

"PRACILLA! Not magilla-Pracilla on the southside? No way homeboy? Tell me it aint' so?"

"And if it is? So what! Look here man, I'm tired of waken up out my sleep with my hand squeezed tight to my dick tryen' to hold back from bursten' all over my self after having a dream about me and Tyra Banks scuba divin' naked in the Bahamas."

"Woooow! Unbelieveable."

"Just be glad your big homie' is gettin' him some. That's all I ask."

"I can respect that but PLEASE make sure you practice safe sex. We don't need you two giants having the largest baby ever born in the Guinness book of world records."

"Are you gone get out and go inside or keep me from enjoyin' my mornin'?"

"Oh, we here already? Good. Look here, I'll hit you up later and don't forget, SAFE SEX!"

"Aiight' Mr. Two-kids instead of one. Now shut my door and holla' back."

CHAPTER 42

"**L**ets get straight to the point here shall we. You haven't said over three words to the man since the last time you dove overboard out on his expensive yacht and now, out the blue, you expectin' him to grant you, a leave, from work, TODAY, on the day of your husband trial?"

"Do I look scared to you?"

"No mamm! Not at all! But on your way out his office when he finally tells you to don't ever look back, can I have that jar of chocolate candy on your desk you been holdin' on to for over a year now? They're very good you know."

"And how would you know? Unless, unless," seeming surprised, "so YOU'RE the one who been stickin' them grimy lil' fingers in my goodies. I was wonderin' why it kept lookin' as if they were decreasin' in size."

"Right now, that's not important. Your job is."

"Which is the main reason for me askin' him. As much as I've done and contributed to this place of business, how can he refuse me? And if that's the case, he won't ever have to worry about tellin' me not to look back at him or his office nor this congested cubicle ever again."

"Will you be serious for once in your life child! The man won't be refusin' your request but your negligence you been practicin' with him for quite some time now. That's where the problem will occur."

"Well, I guess it's time that minor problem comes to an end this very moment," raising up out her seat.

Standing in applause, "That's my girl! I believe in you!"

Shontae wondered if several of her coworkers were in on Naomi's humor witnessing them clap their hands as well.

"WHAT'S ALL THIS COMMOTION ABOUT OUT HERE," yelled Mr. Smith from his office door. "COME ON PEOPLE! Deadlines, deadlines! Legs get back to them!"

She paused and waited for him to close the door.

"Why you stoppin' girl? Remember, you aint' scared!"

"Easier said than done," she mumbled to herself.

The span of silence exercised in the past between them made her wonder if some sort of dislike towards her had been embedded in his mind. She had the slightest of clue on what his reaction might be in the upcoming seconds. His attempts at conversating with her several days ago went ignored. On the night of their rendezvous, it was necessary she escape not only his up and close approach but the sensual feeling she continued experiencing whenever his hand touched hers. The four years of swimming lessons in high school prepared her for a dive that came as a surprise to them both. She viewed land to be no more than a half a mile and calculated just the right amount of water for her to swam across with ease. Her trip back home in a taxi cab was an expensive one but her only option. She wanted no one to grow concern of her absence and promised Miss. Hick of her return by twelve noon.

She barged in his office. He swung around in his chair. Their eyes met. His with anger. Hers with determination.

"Excuse me Mr. Smith but I need to talk with you for a minute."

"But in a rude way? This better be pretty damn good."

"Yes sir, it is." They continued their harden stare. He pointed for her to have a seat. "Mr. Smith, I know things between us in the past haven't been to great. In fact, non-communicative."

"That still didn't stop you from bursting through my door now did it?"

"No sir it didn't but sir, my husband starts trial today and-"

"You mean to tell me he didn't take the plea," displaying a strong sign of concern.

"Unfortunately, he didn't."

"What is he thinkin'?"

"As I was sayen' sir, would it be alright if I took a leave from work for the next couple of days? Or at least until his trial is over."

"Mrs. Hick, you take as much time as you need but only under one condition."

She withheld a response contemplating if he might be up to his ususal salacious behavior.

"Which is?"

"That you stop with the silent treatment long enough to fill me in on how the trial is coming along."

"That can easily be arranged sir." She felt relieved he hadn't held any hard feelings against her viewing the smile on his face. "Thank you."

"No, thank you for speaking to me again."

She barely made it out his office before Naomi crept up from behind.

"Now that's an uncommon look on your face after returning from such a serious situation."

"That's right. It was real brief and straight to the point. I told him what I expected and he politely abided."

"Bullshit woman! You don't run nuthin' round here."

"Except yo' paycheck and if you keep doubtin' me the way you do, I'll be forced to show you just how much I really am in control of your destiny."

"Threats are for those who neglects respect. Now keep playin' with mines."

"Struck a nerve I see."

"Not hardly. Just a moment of me hatin' on you. But one thing still remains."

"And what might that be?"

"Someone STILL has the hot's for you."

"All because he granted me what I deserve?"

"Only because to him, in his own lil' world, you'll always be known as the secret lover he can only dream of having."

"That is a wonderful dream aint' it?'

"Only til' your world slips at the doorstep of a stranger."

"And that'll be a cold day in hell my friend. A cold day in hell."

CHAPTER 43

He waited in a holding tank pacing the floor. A federal agent of similar build laced in a suit and tie along with ray-ban shades greeted Nard cell door for a departure. The trip up the elevator from the first to the ninth floor was but a brief second. Inside the courtroom appeared much more spacious than he envision. Its double-doors swung back and forth with people entering. Two officers stood near the entrance signaling in which direction to be seated. He refused to look back in search of family and friends confident his support was within eyesight.

"ALL RISE!"

In unison, everyone stood in a motionless stature. A pudgy, elderly white man entered from behind a door in a black robe taking a seat at the bench. Nard stood astonished at how the shouted words halted the room minor commotion. Numerous of times on television he witnessed such rehearsed act including the friendly performance recently experienced at home with Mike and M-J. To have actually taken part in the modern judicial ritual meant a last and final chance with changing his mind about going to trial or halt any additional procedures and settle for a plea.

"JUDGE LYNCH NOW PRESIDING OVER THE CASE NUMBER 49-CRL-362-0886, UNITED STATES OF AMERICA VERSUS BERNARD HICK'S IN THE MIDDLE DISTRICT OF GEORGIA! THIS COURTROOM IS NOW IN SESSION! YOU MAY ALL BE SEATED!"

"Okay then," readjusting himself in the large recliner seat, "who would like to proceed first in my courtroom today?"

"That will be me your honor." The lawyer used a forefinger to unloosen the stiff collar from around his neck while strolling the open floor in observance of the curious eyes who impatiently awaited his first word. He held up a finger. "To the people of the jury. To the people of the courtroom.... and to those of a conscious mind. I have only one opening word to begin our session with." He moved from in front of the judge bench over to the jury box. "LIES," controlling the room quietness with his stalling silence again. "Would you believe, or rather COULD you believe, for one minute, that my client sitting over there," pointing at Nard, "just happens to be another victim of poor investigation conducted by both federal and state authorities, once more, spending AND wasting, let us not leave that part out, wasting our tax payers hard earned money and time just for the purpose of trying to convict a man, ANY man who fills such a seat as my client does here today. The opening argument I'm prepared to present to you today in this here courtroom is a definite fact of an individual who has not only been falsely accused of a crime he did not commit but was also abused by the incompetent, intolerable behavior conducted by both officers and agents who participated in this mayhem. To further my client misfortune, they're also here today to present to you insufficient evidence that could possibly be permitted in this here courtroom with the probability of my client not leaving here a free man today. But guess what people... WE," waving a hand above the heads of the jurors, "will not sit and tolerate such injustice in this here courtroom and on that note, the bottom line is this, let not a man stand convicted for his own ignorance of any wrongdoing but for the negligence of his own ability in being more cautious of his actual surrounding. Thank you your honor," taking a seat.

"Bravo, bravo, bravo," clapping his hand, "but must I remind everyone that this is not a comedy show and that there are no cameras rolling on any celebrities in here today." The prosecutor closed a folder on his table taking a stand. "Jurors of the courtroom, let us not forget that an illegal act of crime HAS been committed and before this trial ends, I WILL prove that the defendant had, if not full involvement, partook in some part of wrong doing in one way or the other. Let us all remember this, circumstantial evidence is ALWAYS enough to withhold a conviction in the court of law and in my mind, without an ounce of doubt, a second guess, that the evidence I'm prepared to present to you today will be proven beyond a reasonable doubt guaranteeing anyone who participated in a finding of guilt that our quote-unquote 'tax payers dollars' will in some way have benefitted our society by taking another criminal off the clean streets of Muscogee County. Thank you your honor."

"Well, well, well! Look who finally return. If it aint' the cell-keeper. Do I need to step out a minute so you can embrace everything you miss about your bunk so much?"

"Nah' bra'. You aiight'. I'm just gonna' climb up there and relax a lil'."

"First day was rough I suppose?"

"Draggin'."

"Who ever said it was gonna' be fun. How you lawyer do? He put on the way he's paid to?"

"I guess he did aiight'. Maybe a lil' too much of excessive talkin' I thought but if it sets me free, preach lawyer preach."

"And I bet you the prosecutor played a role that was brief and straight to the point?"

"That's about the size of it."

"I already know. I had one perform the same act at my trial. Very discreet. At least up until the end when my lawyer had run out of bullets and the prosecutor started to shoot everything he had at us takin' his sweet time with hittin' his target. And after that, we went down like Mike Tyson losing his crown in the twelfth round. Guilty on all three charges. They weren't the least bit concern about convicting me for the drugs they found as long as the prosecutor got what he wanted. The rest was a wrap." Three life sentences for the murder of three men who tried robbing him at his home is what he was facing. His lawyer controlled the jurors mind up to the final week of trial when the prosecutor presented two kilograms of crack cocaine found stashed away in the same area the three bodies laid proving the robbers true motives behind their attempt. The lawyer refuted the fact that had it not been for his client quick thinking, he could have been the one murdered. Unfortunately, it was proven at trial that he was a two-time felon, on the run for a parole violation and in possession of an unauthorized fire arm. "And now, here I am. Not only singing jail house blues but I have the rest of my life to pay dues for my society. Some life aint' it.

"It could be worse."

"HA! What could be more worst than someone takin' your freedom away from you until your dead?"

"Forgive me for my thoughtless comment J. My mind is in a state of disarray right now."

"You don't owe me no explanation dawg'. You just tryin' to give me something to smile about."

"If you don't mind celly, I think I'll get me a nap and hope I wake up somewhere far from this dungeon."

"Good luck. Cause the more I wake up here, the more I lose sight of what's happening outside these walls. Just stay focus bra'. You'll be aiight'."

He totally agreed. Even if worse came to worst, he would eventually be going home one day unlike his cell mate who remained trapped inside the belly of the beast for the duration of his life. He cleared the horrible thought from his mind and replaced it with better ones before dozing off.

CHAPTER 44

"**W**as that a long and exhausting trial today or what?"

"I have to agree with you on that honey. I kept dozin' off it seem like every hour on the hour."

"Which could mean only one thing," placing himself on top of her. "Yeah girl! Um-hm! I got you like I like you now! Right between the sheets with big daddy. I knew all I had to do was be patient."

"Aiight' Mike. You got me. Fare and square this time. But before we get started, I got two rules that you must promise to abide by."

Rubbing a hand over her breast in excitement, "Talk to ME baby!"

"The first one is NO PULLEN' on my hair. I just got it done yesterday and it'll be too expensive to have it done all over again. As for the last one which seems to be the most complicated one for you, if you can't last past your usual three seconds then don't EVEN waste your time with gettin' naked. In fact, if you have to, gone off in the bathroom and jack yourself off so you'll be able to take me beyond your normal sprints. Shit, I want me some tonight as bad as you do but yo' ass aint' about to leave me stranded here playin' with my vibrator half the night.

"Quit with the jokes woman and give me some of that good ol' lovin' of yours," kissing her entire face.

"Mom…dad," knocking on their bedroom door, "I need to talk with y'all,"

"I know damn well this aint' happenin' to me! GO AWAY SON! ME AND YOUR MOTHER ARE ASLEEP.!"

"Let's see what the child wants first, Mike. We got all night for you to try and break your three second record."

"And since when you started back being so concern with our son problems? You just started having dinner with us at the same table."

"Regardless of how stupid he might act at times, he's still my child. COME IN SON!"

"Mom, dad, their's something important I need to discuss with y'all."

"At," grabbing hold of his watch from off the night stand, "twelve in the mornin'? It betta' be a life and death situation."

"Life, yes. Death, only if I hang myself."

"Yeah, well, that can possibly be arranged, but what's on your mind? And make it quick! The mornin' just started and me and your mother are about to act like two alcoholics up in here."

"That's disgusting pops'."

"What's wrong son," asked Shenequa.

"Their's a secret I've been hiden' from ya'll. Basically everyone. Including myself at times but not anymore because they're startin' to show a lil' bit."

Placing her back against the head board, "They! And just whom and what are you referrin' to as they?"

"Remember that day I was caught in the wrong place at the wrong time about seven months ago."

"Just as sure as I kicked you out."

"Well, how would you feel if I told y'all that you two are soon to be potential grandparents?"

"GRANDPARENTS," shouting together.

"Sound crazy don't it."

"Comin' from you and your past history, not hardly child," stated Shenequa.

"You mean to sit here and tell me son that you got BOTH of them pregnant at the same time?"

"I believe so dad."

"What did they mother had to say about all this?"

"They haven't said anything to their parents that they're pregnant by the same man and judging by the looks of things, they probably never will."

"And whose gonna' be responsible for raising the two because you sure as hell aint' got no job."

"I'm workin' on that right now as we speak momma'."

"And how many times have I heard that lie before?"

"More than we can imagine baby and that's fa' sure."

"I mean, can you believe this Mike? Our son, our only son, a soon-to-be father with barely a pot to piss in and a window to throw it out of. I would hate to ask you what was you thinkin' at the time but if I aint' mistakin', it looks to me as if you, once again, left yo' wallet AND brain somewhere in El Sagando."

"So what do you plan on doin' now?"

"Whateva' it is dad, I betta' do it quick cause the babies aren't too far off from delivery."

"Lord, Jesus, PLEASE give me the strength I need to continue claiming this child as my own."

"You see what you done went and did son? Got your mother all roused up. Let us talk this over for a while tonight and we'll see you with a better plan first thing in the mornin'. Don't go runnin' off with your friends or anything tomorrow. Just hang tight and we'll go from there."

"Thank y'all for being understanding."

"Not understanding but non-violent. The same thing that keeps me from burying you alive out in the backyard."

"In the mornin' son. Goodnight."

"Goodnight dad, Mom."

"Um-hm," she stated non-chalantly.

"I know I was wild when I was a child comin' up but JUNIOR, junior surpasses my foolishness with flyen' colors."

"Even if income wasn't the issue, that boy knows damn well he aint' responsible enough to see about no child and to think, TWO of them."

"So what do we do now?"

"Simple. We sleep on it," stretching her limbs out underneath the covers.

"Not so fast young lady. We got some unfinished business to attend to."

"I know we do honey but right now mommy' can hardly even focus after what he just told us and I want to be able to put my all into pleasing you big daddy."

"To be honest with you", cuddling up with her, "and though it might sound crazy comin' from me, but I feel the same damn way. Junior problems done took the fight out of me to."

"I'm sorry baby."

"Gone and get your rest young lady. There's always tomorrow."

CHAPTER 45

TRIAL: DAY TWO (2)

"Now, Mr. Marc Rolllins, would you mind, without excluding a single detail, explain to the jury on exactly how it all went down on the day of the incident sir?"

"Real simple. I had asked Nard-"

"Excuse me sir, when you say Nard, exactly whom are you referring to?"

"He's right there behind you to your left."

"You mean the gentleman sitting beside Mr. Quirk, the attorney, over at the small table?"

"Yes sir."

"Let it be known for the record that my witness has clearly identified Mr. Bernard Hick's as the person he is referring to as Nard. Alright then Mr. Rollins, you may proceed with sharing the details."

"Like I said, I had asked Nard to ride with me for lunch break. Shortly along the way I explained to him that I needed to make a quick stop at a house in the direction we were travelin' in and he stated 'cool'."

"Cool as in alright? In agreeance?"

"Yes sir."

"During the time of y'all traveling, did you ever once mention your reason for makin' the stop while en route of something to eat?"

Glancing in Nard's direction, "Yes sir...I did."

"THAT'S A LIE YOUR HONOR!"

"MR. HICK, in my courtroom, there will be no such outburst like that tolerated! This is your ONLY warning. The next time, you'll be placed under a gag order. Am I makin' myself clear Mr. Hick's?"

"But sir, the man is lyin'!"

"Lets let the jury decide that for us young man. Mr. Quirk, he's your responsibility."

"Yes sir your honor. We clearly understand you." Whispering in his ear, "Let me handle anymore outburst from now on Mr. Hick."

"My bad Quirk but the man just sat up there and told a bold-face lie."

"We'll get'em. Have patience."

"Do you mind if I proceed Mr. Quirk?" He lifted a thumb at the prosecutor signaling for a continuation. "Mr. Rollins, would you mind finishing your statement?"

"Yes sir. I clearly explained to Nard that I was about to make a pick-up of some artillery and for him to be the lookout man for me while I went inside."

"I object your honor! The witness statement is based on all lies as well as coerced!"

"Mr. Quirk, the witness has fair grounds to explain his side of the story as much as your client does. You'll have your chance to cross-examin him. Okay Mr. Emerson, you may proceed."

"Thank you your honor. Mr. Rollins, at any point did Mr. Hick refuse to partake in such illegal activity?"

"No sir. He didn't."

"So let me get this straight, you mean to say that Mr. Hick just remain seated in the front seat of your car, as a witness, without any such denial or refusal of an actual crime in progress and hung around all the way through or at least until the agents and police arrived?"

"Yes sir. That is correct."

"And exactly how long were you inside before the house was raided by both state and federal agencies?"

"No more than seven or eight minutes."

"Were there anyone else riding in the car with you two?"

"No sir."

"No other accomplice?"

"No sir."

"I have no further questions for the witness your honor. Thank you."

Mr. Quirk wasted no time with approaching the witness.

"Mr. Rollins, do you mind me asking you a question? A rather minute one I should say?"

"No sir. Not at all."

"Have you every drunk a beer before?"

"I object your honor! This has nothing to do with the case at hand here sir."

"Sustain. Mr Quirk, get to the point."

"Your honor, I'm only tryen' to show bad character here. Now, as I was sayin', Mr. Rollins, I've discovered several reports of you going through rehabilitation for alcohol abuse which led to a divorce, loss of job in the past and correct me if I'm wrong here but most alcholics are people that's more than likely mad with the world or either themselves. Is that true Mr. Rollins?"

"In a sense. I guess you can say that?"

"Mr. Rollins, has my client ever cause you any harm in the present or past before?"

"Yeah' he did, to be exact. When we first got locked up together down in the intake at the county jail when he swung on me sir."

"But that was due to an incarceration that could've easily been avoided had someone done the right thing then but beside his behavior for violence, has my client been known as a good samaritan since you first me him?"

"I would think so. Yeah."

"Mr. Rollins, you have done a wonderful job sir. Thank you. And thank you too your honor." He stopped midway to approaching his seat. "I almost forgot one thing your honor," making his way back to the witness stand. "Just one …. last …. simple question." He studied the witness face up close. "Mr. Rollins…are you soon to be release from prison because of your lies?"

"THIS IS ABSURD! Mr. Quirk still continues to wonder off into left field with no apparent reason your honor!"

"I totally agree with you Mr. Emerson which is why this court is going to take a recess so Mr. Quirk can get himself, along with his client, on the right page before they both are banned from my courtroom for wasting my time as well as the courtroom. Mr. Quirk?"

"Yes, your honor?"

"When you return, you better have your A-game present or receive an F, as in FINISHED with this trial leaving your client locked up behind bars without ever having the opportunity with presenting his case."

"Again, your honor, I apologize for our unprofessional behavior and we will return with a much better presentation."

Mallet pointed at him, "You better! This court is now in recess."

TRIAL: <u>CONTINUATION OF DAY TWO (2)</u>

"ALL RISE! This courtroom is now in session!"

"Mr. Quirk, I think we'll start with you and that improved behavior of yours first. I'm pretty sure some arrangements have been made because I'm just DYING to see them."

"Yes sir, your honor," adjusting his tie while in humor of the judge remark. "A breath of fresh air does anybody mind good but if you don't mind sir, I now would like to call the executive chief of A.T.F,. Agent Trano to the witness stand." He studied Trano's hoary appeal in admiration of his short, dominant demeanor. "Mr. Trano, were not you the head agent overseeing this gun bust?"

"Yes sir. That is true."

"And your gun bust involving my client stem from a prior gun bust which the individual involved in that case turned government informant for you that resulted in the seizure of Mr. Rollins, in a house, purchasing some guns that weren't registered nor authorized to be in his possession?"

"That's about the size of it. I couldn't have said it any more planer," smiled Trano.

"Mr. Trano, you have a long work history from starting off as a local police officer and moving up the ladder to becoming one of the top chief in the A.T.F. department."

"I've worked my butt of for my job title! Dedicated many overtime and sleepless nights. Even left my family wondering will I ever make it back home. But fortunately, life goes on and so do I."

"We're not doubting that sir. It's pretty obvious how," rushing over to his table retrieving several sheets of stapled paper, "successful your work history has been with locking up criminals judging by what's in my hand but there was something I saw or rather a few things I read that sort of left me baffled. Mr. Trano, would you have any problem with explaining to the jury how, in the past, you were once facing federal charges for planting drugs on a local drug dealer you were after several years ago that somehow managed to keep evading your drug bust when unexpectedly, at the beginning phases of YOUR trial, the young man just up and disappeared only never to be seen again? Or what about the investigation you were placed under ten years ago involving $50,000's taken out of the confiscating room at the local narcotics task force office that happened on your shift? Care to enlighten us about it sir?"

"Son," face hardening up, "exactly what are you insinuating here? That I might've had something to do with his disappearance or the stolen money? Those are some serious accusation you're accusing me of. Say what you need to say son."

"The name is Mr. Quirk sir. Thank you very much. Now that we have that understood, judging by the facts, it's funny how the kid was never seen again nor were you convicted or even tried in the court of law for that matter. You tell me Mr. Trano. Should my client be worried for his life?"

"If he hasn't done anything wrong it would seem to me that he has nothing to fret about."

"I have nothing further for the witness your honor."

"What about you Mr. Emerson," asked the judge.

"No sir your honor. I have no questions for the witness sir."

"Your honor, since Mr. Emerson has no further questions, I would like to call my last and final witness to the stand. Mr. Bernard Hick, would you mind taking the stand?" His lawyer advised him of the harm testifying might cause. By not defending himself, Nard figured it would do more harm than good leaving the jurors to wonder if he's concealing something. He wanted this chance! If impacting a single juror mind in to believing his innocence was all it took, Nard figured by telling the truth it would only strengthen his chance at prevailing. "How are you feeling today Mr. Hick?"

"Aiight'. I guess."

"If you don't mind Mr. Hick, lets start off by hearing your version of this horrific scenario you've been placed in."

"I mean, there's really not much to explain. Mr. Rolllins went inside the house. I stayed in the car and had dozed off which was partially due to a hangover I experienced the night before and before long, I heard some loud, tapping sound on the window woke me out my slumber. When I looked around to see what it was, that's when I noticed these big letters on some shirts that surrounded me and the car."

"And exactly what was written on some of the shirts?"

"A.T.F."

"And do you know what those three letters mean?"

"Yes sir. Alcohol, Tobacco and Firepower."

"In the process of you and Mr. Rollins traveling together, did he ever mention his reason to you for stopping by the house?"

"Not to my knowledge. No sir."

"What about before you entered his car?"

"Not at all."

"And how long have you known Mr. Rollins?"

"About as long as I've been working for Mercedes Benz Car Dealership."

"Which would be?"

"I'd have to say around eight, maybe nine years."

"And between those years, the two of you never experienced any bad times or anything in you two relationship?"

"Not once."

"So you've treated him like a brother for the most part?"

"Basically."

"Mr. Hick, before I finish with you, what exactly would you like for the jury to know about you sir?"

"Well, I'm not a bad guy. Never committed a crime. I have a college degree. A family man. Everything a productive life should consist of but unfortunately for me being at the wrong place at the wrong time, my carelessness has cost me dearly. Time that can't be changed or erased and sometimes, those are the breaks that life has to offer us. What I have to say to the jurors of the courtroom is this: They say that the truth can set a person free. And hopefully, that truth will weigh more in favor of what is right in the court of law here today. This is too serious of a situation to allow it to be swept under a rug. We can't afford for a costly mistake like this to go unnoticed only to notice it years later after having left permanent life scars on an innocent man and with that being said, if I haven't simplified my justifiable freedom today, well, throw away the key and by all mean…don't ever bother me again."

"Thank you Mr. Hick. I have nothing further your honor."

Mr. Emerson remain stationed in his seat.

"Mr. Hick, you do realize where you're at today don't you?"

"Of course. I'm in a courtroom."

"And you do understand what takes place in this here room don't you?"

"Certainly."

"So you are familiar with the procedures of a lawyer proving a man innocence and a prosecutor, such as myself, convicting the accused?"

"Yes sir."

"Do you realize what the percentage rate of our, particularly the government, convictions throughout the United Stated is?"

"No sir."

"How bout' I throw a round-about figure at you like, maybe 95, 96% conviction rate. Maybe slightly higher."

"That's a lot."

"No Mr. Hick, that's almost ALL of those who enter through the double doors of this room. Now, my question to you is, what makes you so special, different from the rest all because you poured your precious little heart and soul out hoping to receive in return some type of sympathy or passion? Do you realize how many times those exact same words have been spoken in this oak-filled courtroom that surrounds us at this very moment? Mr. Hick," taking a stance in the center floor, "look around you. I would like to welcome you to the real world sir where dreams easily fade away and courtrooms are made every day. You're not a saint Mr. Hick. Not judging by your earlier testimony. You said it yourself that the night before the incident you awoke with a hangover the next morning. I'm sure you were referring to the usage of alcohol. Is that correct?"

"Something like that."

"Yes? No?"

"Yes."

"In order for it to have been considered a quote/unquote 'hangover', your consumption of a certain type of alcohol must was pretty heavy?"

"I had a few bottles of beer along with a glass or two of Bom Bay."

"That would be alcohol AND liquor. Mr. Hick, were you experiencing some sort of trouble at the time?"

"My grandmother had a slight stroke while I was with her earlier that evening and it sort of shook me up pretty bad."

"Bad enough for you to go out and get drunk. Is this a regular trait for you to practice whenever life shakes you up Mr. Hick?"

"This was the first. I'm not a heavy drinker at all."

"But you do drink on occasions I suppose?"

"Every now and then with a few associates of mines."

"Exactly where did this heavy consumption of yours occur?"

"At a friends place of business."

"While open?"

"No sir. It was close."

"So you slept it off inside some ones business?"

"Not really. I managed to drive myself home."

"While heavily intoxicated. That was quite a dangerous task you pulled off Mr. Hick. Endangering the lives of our citizens, driving while under the influence and the list goes on. After awakening that morning, I'm quite sure you experienced some type of headache or something?"

"Definitely."

"Were you clearly conscious of Mir. Rollins informing you on y'all pick-up that morning?"

"I OBJECT YOUR HONOR!"

"Sustain."

"Okay, how about this Mr. Hick since it is clear to the courtroom that you are capable of committing a crime, why didn't you just inform the police of your friend illegal activity?"

"Like I said, I had no actual knowledge of what my so-call friend was doing at the time. As far as I'm concern, it was none of my business."

"If you would have known of a crime being committed, would you had informed some one?"

"Hell nah' man! I mean, no sir. That's snitchin'."

"And you see something wrong with an American citizen informing the authority of a crime possibly being committed?"

"Not if it actually involves that person whose life is in serious danger or someone tryin' to harm the innocent. Other than that, if a man commits a crime, it's only right that he should do the time. Wouldn't you agree?"

"Agree! But without informants, how else would we be able to infiltrate a major gun smuggler or drug trafficking ring or even a cartel without some sort of inside connect? One day Mr. Hick, you will hopefully learn in life that everyone has a position to fill. Some for the good and others for the, well, not so good. But that's life! And life can be very unpredictable at times Mr. Hick. There was a slang used earlier in this courtroom and it went something like this, 'fake it, til' you make it,' I think that was it and with that being said, now I clearly understand what he meant. Sometimes, the truth is never revealed but whose fault is it? Yours? Mine? Anybody? Who knows! Think about it Mr. Hick. I have nothing further your honor."

"Do we have any further witness that both parties would like to cross examine?"

"No sir your honor."

"I second that your honor," concurred Mr. Emerson.

"Alright then, since there are no further witnesses to call, which one of you gentlemen would like to begin with their closing argument first?"

"That'll be me your honor," stated Mr. Quirk taking his usual position beside the jury box. "Who would dare believe for one minute that this trial, this one particular trial, over the past two days, built on the foundation of untold truth, supported by a man of criminal history, criminal intent, BOTH sown from a criminal mind, could possibly impact a single juror into believing any of his gibberish with trying to destroy, for unknown selfish motives, the life and innocent times of my client? FABRICATION," he emphasized loud and clear, "if permitted, does only one thing to our humanity." He retrieved a dollar bill from within his slacks holding it up as high as he could pacing back and forth for everyone to view. "It tears," ripping the note in half, "the core strength of our judicial system apart. And if WE, the sovereign being of the United States of America, permit such a destruction to occur then where does that leave the history of our founding fathers 'LIBERTY, JUSTICE and the PURSUIT of HAPPINES' existing in today's strengthening trend of deceit…dishonesty…and deception? Obviously then it'll be safe for me to say that life as we know it has little, if ANY, meaning on this God-given planet. So why not just go about living it in a reclusive state? Seems to me like the only possible way to avoid most of the horrific activities taking place outside our homes. OOOR…how bout' rewriting history today at this very moment by utilizing the power everyone in this courtroom has been granted by saving a man's life from a lifetime of pain for having placed his life at the mercy of the juror, in prayer and hopes, for someone, ANYONE, to identify with the truth he has presented in this courtroom here today. Judging by the lack of credibility and facts involved in this case, I would like to think that my client prayers has already been answered. I now leave you with one more thought in mind: 'FORGIVE ME' says the accused but to forget me leaves the accused stranded with know…where…to go. Thank you your honor."

Mr. Emerson wasn't expecting an ending speech so in depth. Maybe something more of a weaker content might've described Mr. Quirk attributes but bad judgement once before almost caused him to lose out on a high profile case. His first to be exact. Based on the information gathered against his opponent, the inexperienced lawyer was not only reported to have been naïve but a public defender also. Mr. Emerson informed himself of no reason in over exerting his skills. Just stick to the basics he practiced throughout most of law school. Big mistake! The trial ended up being a hung jury all because of his key witness refusal in speaking under oath at the last minute. A man he never consulted with up until his first question asked at the witness stand. "I plea the fifth Mr. Emerson." From that point on, he made it a duty to consult with all witnesses first prior to testifying at trial.

"Mr. Emerson, will you be presenting your closing argument anytime soon or drafting out an essay on paper?"

"Yes sir! Yes sir your honor. I'm coming as we," scribbling down a final line on paper "SPEAK!" He went and placed his back against the front of the judges bench. "To begin my closing argument FIRST by commenting on the remark of 'Justice, Liberty and the Pursuit of Happiness,' Mr. Quirk mentioned of shortly ago…YES, those are words equivalent to where our judicial system remains today and YES, justice will always be balanced out by the scale of what's right and what's wrong in a court of law. But by allowing ourselves to give up faith in what has lasted for hundreds and hundreds of years means a MAJOR change in history that's more than likely to fail at exceeding where I am standing or where you are seated and quite frankly, I'm very content with how America, the land of the free as well as the home of the brave, exist in the world today. To touch up on the facts that were presented is simple: Guilt that was proven beyond a reasonable doubt! We've presented physical evidence capable of mass destruction but on a minor level, seized in the possession of Mr. Rollins, agents who testified to arresting Mr. Hick while seated outside the home as the lookout man inside a parked car and furthermore, the actual testimony of Mr. Rollins clearly alleging of Mr. Hick partial involvement pertaining to their illegal activity. Now, for me to continue on with a scenario outside of the scope on what was actually proven today would no doubt, in my mind, do more harm than good possibly confusing the jurors and that, by far, would be considered the tail that wags the dog.

"In satisfying the criteria of aiding and abetting, one must have assisted with another person's act of crime but in this case, in violation of the law and by sparing Mr. Hick with the chance of being found not guilty would indeed prove that we do have a serious flaw in our legal system. One that's waaaay beyond repair. But what weight of a thought, a spoken word has against actual facts? Judging by the scale of justice, I would have to say that a feather in the hand ways less than a grain of sand cause that's EXACTLY what all the facts will have amounted to today if the wrong decision is handed down. By all means jurors of the court, do what you must but remember one thing, a child, an innocent child, is gun down once, sometimes twice a day, by a stray bullet. Think about it. Thank you your honor."

"All right then. Being that all arguments are finalized. We'll go into recess long enough to allow the jury enough time to deliberate on a verdict. Jury of the court, take as much time needed. No one is rushing any of you. This is a serious scenario you all are involved with. The power of your vote can either imprison or free a man but whatever decision you make, let it be, in your heart, the right one. I also would like to advise the people of the courtroom not to wander off to far. In other words, go out and stretch your limbs, take a break, anything you desire but return as soon as possible. The deliberation usually takes up to a few hours or maybe even longer, depending on the facts of a case. So this is what we'll do, the time now is 4 p.m. Will go into recess until further notice," slamming his mallet down.

"My son did pretty dam good on that witness stand. I see life has went and taught him a few things along the way after all."

"Lets just hope it was convincing enough for the jury to decide in his favor Ms. Hick. As much as I hate to say this, the government drives a hard bargain with anybody. They prefer to have a person mind, body and soul over all the money in the world."

"The prosecutor didn't really present no hard evidence. Just a bunch of lies."

"ALL lies! But like he said, words alone can get a man a life sentence up in here."

"You're right about that Mike. This justice system doesn't play fair at all," mentioned Shontae.

"I think your husband will be alright young lady. I got this strong gut feelin'."

Miss Hick patted her on the back in hopes of comforting her daughter-in-law worries.

"For the family sake, I hope you're right Miss Hick."

"Would you ladies like to go out and get a bite to eat?"

"No thank you child. I'm not missing a thing. Not until the jury comes back with their final decision for my son. I'm aiight'. I got a few cheese crackers in my purse that I can sneak around to nibbling on."

"No thank you Mike. I think I'll wait here with Miss Hick also."

"What about you Shenequa? Care to take a walk with me?"

"Yeah. Why not. I could definitely use a break from lookin' at all these devils in a suit and tie all day."

"We'll be back shortly everyone."

The congested cell came equipt with a toilet and metal stool half the size of a chair. A location that shared no outside light nor a window on the door for him to view out of. Nard remembered J-Dub description quite clear of the small room he called 'The Box'. Inmates sanction for violent acts back at the county jail were held inside one for their punishment indefinitely. No other holding cell existed on the ninth floor. Maybe the sole purpose for having been placed there was to weaken him into a state of submission. To try forcing him in admitting some type of guilt. His escorter noticed the slight worry expressed across his face seconds before approaching the cell door. "Home, sweet home...for now" josh the guard. The racing thoughts he struggled with soon subsided hoping it all ended on a positive note or two. The first being removed from the box and the second one a "get-out-of-jail-free' verdict. A thought he felt relieved to have experienced.

The long hours of trial had left him feeling drained. Getting some rest was all he could really think of. A torn mat on the floor forced him to tough it out on the stool instead. Regardless of the outcome today, he felt pleased knowing he fought long and hard against the government for what he believed in. More than what he could say for many other young men at the county jail who were either afraid of the courthouse 97% conviction rate or just lacked the courage in defending for themselves. Regardless of how much he tried sympathizing with the scenario, it still made no sense to him at all.

"AIIGHT' MR. HICK," sliding a key into the slot unlocking the door, "it's time."

"ALL RISE! This courtroom is now in session! You may be seated!"

"Okay then, now that everyone has returned as I asked of you, have the jury decided on a verdict?"

"Yes sir, we have your honor."

"Good. Will you please read it aloud to the court room.?"

"In the case of United States v. Bernard Hick's, we the jury, find Bernard Hick's, the defendant-

"HOLD ON YOUR HONOR! WAIT ONE MINUTE!"

"ORDR! ORDER," pounding his mallet. "MISS, ARE YOU INSANE!"

"Just one minute your honor," approaching his bench. Several officers responded immediately by taking hold of her arms and placing them in back of her. "Just give me one minute judge. Just one measly minute."

"Alright! Alright. Let her go. But don't you come any closer then where you are at."

"Thank you judge," shoving some space between her and the officers. "Judge, your honor-"

"Don't do this momma'! Don't embarrass me like this!"

"Shut up boy! I don't know what you talkin' about but I'm tryin' to get yo' butt home. Now, as I was sayin your honor, my son aint' no crook, no criminal, convict, none of the three C's in a jailhouse. He didn't have nothing to do with those guns your honor. My son doesn't even like guns. When he was born, the first thing God did was gave him a brain to use not bullets."

"Get to the point mamm! It's been a long day and we're all tryin' to get out of here.

"You aint lyin' bout' that judge. I got some pork rinds boiling on the-"

"MAMM!"

"Oh, I'm sorry sir. But anyway, my son is innocent. Point blank. No ifs, ands or buts about it. It should be real simple with solving this case and that's by freeing an innocent man. There you have it sir. Jury, you may carry on. Sorry bout' the disturbance judge but you know how mothers are about their children. Especially this black woman."

Shaking his head, "Please mam, would you have a seat."

"Sure thing judge."

"Now, where was I?"

"They were getting ready to free my son your honor!"

"Yes, yes. I can handle it from here mam. Jurors of the court, would you try and finish what was so rudely interrupted right before you read aloud the verdict?"

"Yer sir your honor. We the jury finds Bernard Hick's...GUITLY as charged!"

"I KNOW DAMN WELL," yelled Miss. Hick.

"Would somebody grab hold of her and escort her out my courtroom!"

"DON'T WORRY SON," tussling with the officers who placed her in handcuffs, "I'LL BE BACK TO BURST YOU OUT! I PROMIIIIIISE," she shouted on her way out the door.

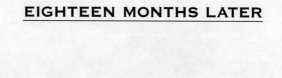

EIGHTEEN MONTHS LATER

CHAPTER 46

The C.O. unlocked the cell door. Nard hopped down off the bunk. Repeated words of, "Wha a' gwaan bredren, wha a' gwaan," spoken in the background meant Red-Eyes, his Jamaican cellmate, was wide alert. The first few weeks were slightly complicated understanding a foreign lingo. Though as time progressed, Nard's interpretation improved tremendously.

Inquisitive stares greeted his entrance inside the day room. Rarely did he strike up a conversation this early in the day for unknowing the mood one might've woke up in. A nodding gesture walking pass several inmates signified the feeling was mutual.

"CHOOOOW CAAALL," yelled the C.O.

The fleeing crowd rushed out the unit. In no haste, Nard trailed knowing breakfast seldom changed from its normal routine of coffee cake or corn flake cereals. Fruit included. An item which required a stoppage before heading out to recreation.

"YO' NARD! WAIT UP PIMPY! LET A YOUNG PLAYA' HOLLA' AT'CHA!"

The familiar sound of Bruh's voice prepared him for a discussion of either women, drugs or thugs. Topics he wanted nothing to partake in this early in the morning. He attempted a swift escape inside contemplating on how wrong of him it would be evading his closest associate. Bruh knew of no one other than Nard he could relate to. They were the only two from Columbus at a federal correctional institution in Jessup, Georgia which held a little over fifteen hundred inmates from different parts of the world. Prior discussion about home exposed them to some of the same people they once had close ties with in the past. Though living in separate housing units, one always found time to socialize with the other at least once a day.

Nard watched on as his friend neared. Possibly one to two inches taller weighing two hundred and fifty pounds. Not a single ounce of body fat. The closer he approached, the lesser of a view he permitted around his frame.

"Guess what pimpy," slightly exhausted from hurrying to catch up.

"Not right now Bruh'. Nor right now. Too early in the morning."

"I know it is and good mornin' to you too sir."

"Good mornin' big homie."

"Look here pimpy', I got a letter yesterday from baby-momma talkin' bout' it's cool for me when I get out to come live with her."

"That's a good thing. I'm proud of you Bruh'."

"A GOOD THING! Maaan', that bitch aint' hollered at me for the last seven years I been gone. But see, I know what it is. She think she's slick. I'm willing to bet you she done got word about the future change in the crack law that's about to free my ass and she calls herself tryin' to put in first bid on ol' Bruh'. I mean, I aint' mad at her for leaving me to rot in the jungle but DAM, how she gone try and come at me sideways like that? She could've at least sent me a card or two. A lil' bit of money. Something to show some sign of concern. The woman aint' even bring my lil' girl down to see me. Now that's what you call cold-blooded."

Not half as cold-blooded as Nard remembered of his friend having no knowledge of his life being in serious danger a while back. Bruh' drinking habit had somehow managed to exceed his spending limit with a large amount of debt owed out. Through a reliable source, Nard was informed of the trouble awaiting Bruh's return from visit one afternoon. He quickly consulted with the three men in attempt of resolving things in a friendlier manner. "Look here…PARTNA'! You need to come up with $300's ASAP if you plan on saving your friends ass. No shawt' chain either!" "I tell you what gentlemens," spoke Nard, "how bout' I western union you $250's before my friend return from visit?" They huddled together for a brief second with one finally responding, "That'll work! But anything late of

3 o'clock and guess what?" The shortest one standing maybe five-foot six who did most of the talking lifted his shirt displaying what appeared like a shank tucked halfway down his pants. Just as he promised, the money made it in perfect time and not a minute to late. He caught up with Bruh' coming out of visit.

"Bruh', let me ask you a serious question?"

"What's up pimpy'? Talk to me."

"First thing first, how was visit? Did you enjoy yourself?"

"Ah' man, it was sweet! Mom. Daughter. That girl is getting big. Just like her daddy."

"Good, good, good. Now, I don't mean to sound crazy by asking you this but are you familiar with death?"

"With death! What kind of question is that? I guess so. Yeah. A funeral of some sort."

"Then what exactly would you like for me to put on your tombstone once you're dead and gone cause that's exactly what was about to take place over fifteen minutes ago."

"Quit playin' man. Now who in the world want me dead at this soft ass prison? Aint' nobody tryin' to kill big Bruh'."

"Prince. Big C. Kutty. Ring a bell?" His jaw slumped. Head soon followed. "Don't worry Bruh'. This time, it's on me but I'll share this with you, I'm not gonna' always be around to save you. So as of today, starting now, this needs to be the day you begin saving yourself. You're a grown man Bruh'. So try and handle your business like one before your business handles you like a child."

He felt more ashamed than startled knowing someone had informed Nard about his bad habit getting the best of him promising to pay it all back. Nard accepted the repayment but without the interest he tried offering him. Bruh' discontinued the drinking for good, a decision that strengthen their bondage as time pass.

"Pimpy'! Pimpy'," waving a hand in front of his face, "you aint' even payin' me no attention."

"I was. I was just checkin' out that fine ass lieutenant making her way down here to the dining hall."

Peering over his shoulder, "You mean Ms. Cooper. For an officer, she is kind of bad. Red bone at that. Shawt'. Jet black curly hair. Pretty face.

Nice round ass in place. For an ol' cougar, I'll definitely have to say she got it goin' on."

"You know what they say don't you? Better with age will always make the front page."

"But like I was tellin' you earlier, I can't see it. No way. I'll write her back lettin' her know thanks, but no thanks."

"Just try not to spread any dislike towards your baby-momma around your daughter to much. Keep it as positive as possible. Even when you don't want to."

"Good morning genltemens," she stated indifferently.

"Good mornin' Ms.…..Coooooper."

"THOMAS JONES," halting her entrance, "boy, you better not be around here bullying my compound again."

"I'm not Ms. Coooooper."

"And what's wrong with your friend staring at me with that harden look on his face Mr. Jones? He acts as if he never seen a lady before."

"I haven't," defending himself. "Not with such grace and a gorgeous face as yours."

"A gorgeous face you don't say? Why thank you for the compliment sir. Now, if you don't mind, how about having a seat up there on that bench in front of the lieutenant office and we'll see how well I spell out gorgeous on the incident report you're about to receive."

"Ahhh' Ms. Cooper. My friend aint' mean no harm by it."

"You aiight' Bruh'. I can handle it. I got myself into this and I damn well better know how to get myself out of it."

As ordered, he waited on the bench for her return. The dining hall closed a short while ago, pissed off he was unable to grab a fruit. Her presence soon appeared. The closer she approached, the more her beauty captivated his mind. She instructed him to follow her inside.

"Close my door and have a seat Mr. Flirtatious." She fed several goldfish in a small fish tank atop of a filing cabinet. "With grace and a gorgeous face," taking a seat at her desk. "Tell me, what exactly were you thinking sir?"

"I wasn't mamm."

"It's okay to call me Ms. Cooper. Mamm makes me feel like I'm gettin'" ol'." She was forty-five and not a single trace of it showed on her face. "And what's your name young man?"

"Bernard Hick."

"I usually can remember names by faces but yours is sort of unfamiliar to me."

"I'm not the type with over exposing myself. Low-key and out of staff and inmates way."

"That's an excellent method of staying out of trouble. Maybe that's why I'm not too familiar with your face."

"That can only mean I'm makin' both our lives easy."

"Up until you felt the need to express how beautiful I am."

"Didn't mean no harm with being real Ms. Cooper."

"None taken'. But don't you think there's a better way in complimenting what you admire without being so open about it?"

"Certainly."

"Then prove it."

"You mean, here? Right now?"

"What's wrong with that? There's nobody in the office but us two. Don't tell me you've gotten scared? What ever happened to that so-call 'bold man' who was standing outside the dining hall? Where did he go?"

"He's right here but how do I know that you're not tryen' to set me up?"

"If that was the case, all I would have to do is hit this here red button on my walkie-talkie and when staff arrive just inform them of your salacious behavior. It's that simple."

He searched her eyes carefully. Her return stare was mutual.

"And anyway, what sense would it make to repeat myself twice when it's obvious that the whole dam compound dreams about you day and night?"

"Was that your slick way of flirting with me again sir?"

"Only if you can keep up."

"I'll take that as a challenge Mr. Hick," standing to her feet. "You probably have bit off more than you can chew young man."

"As long as it's well-done, season properly and admires my eating technique," making his way towards the door, "I can chew on it all the way up to the point where she…"

He placed a finger up to his mouth. She mimicked his action watching the door close behind him.

The gravel track at recreation revealed fewer walkers than anticipated. It permitted him some quiet time while seeking a piece of mind. He dwelt on Shontae's discomfort detected during their recent visit. Those three to four trips to visit him monthly were over eight hours on each occasion. She mentioned nothing to him of the strain it caused. When questioned about it she replied, "Baby, I'm okay. Don't worry. I'll be fine." To continue enquiring of her distress would do more harm than good and decided it was best if he dismissed the topic altogether. He informed her to take some time off from visiting him for a month or so. She refused.

Before his arrival at the assigned federal prison to serve out his sentence, Nard struggled with how to inform his kids of his whereabouts. Nothing bothered him more than having to sit down and look his kids in their eyes and explain to them as to why their father won't be returning home with them. That day had finally presented itself over a year ago. On their first trip to visit him his son asked Shontae as to why there were so many barb-wired fences surrounding the building. "It's a prison stupid," responded his sister. "Mrs. Hick, is my daddy in prison," asked Kedar. Shontae refused to answer any of his questions wishing they'd hurried up and made it inside.

Nard caught a glimpse of their entrance. Neither of his kids appeared any different from the last time he saw them as a free man. They rushed over to where he sat, hugging him for dear life. Loud cries alarmed him of their pain and hurt. "Now, now my kids. Calm down, calm down. It's gonna' be alright. Daddy's here." He settled them down and took their seats. Before visit ended, he instructed his son in taking care of both families while he's away. Kedar glanced up, teary eyed, agreeing to uphold his father orders.

He made it back to the housing unit. Showered. One of the four sets of brown Dickies outfit issued for work detail was laid out on the bunk. Freshly pressed. His mother and grandmother was arriving any minute for a visit. He informed them over the phone last night not to worry so much about his well-being. The long ride didn't sit well with him at all. Grandma laughed at his spoken buffoonery. The same way he catered to her in the past, she felt obligated to return the favor by being at his side no matter where they sent him. Mrs. Hick consulted with the family doctor first to determine if riding back and forth on the highway with her mother would have some type of side effects on her condition. He explained of none but requested she drink plenty of water along with stretching her limbs every so often.

The unit officer slid open his cell door. Nard signaled for one more minute sliding on a pair of institution boots. Saturday visits held the largest gathering. He knew finding a seat would be difficult the longer he took with getting dressed. The large room was just as he predicted. Some adults were forced to remain standing next to where their family sat. Even the designated room for kids to play in was overcrowded. He walked out onto the patio spotting his mother waving hand at a table far off in the corner.

"Hello young ladies," hugging them both. "Now y'all know how much I dislike you two travelin' on the highway without any male supervision."

"As your great, famous mother would say, 'Son, we're grown'. Oh my lord! I can't believe I just said that. Your mother is finally startin' to rub off on me but in the wrong way. Let me hurry up and get back to my normal self again. How you been doin' son?"

"I'm good grandma'. Just good. And you?"

"Besides being bossed around by you know who, I could complain but I won't. I'll just say this, son…PLEASE hurry home and come get your mother cause she is driving me CRAZY back home. Every time I look around she's demanding this or requesting that. All I ask of that child is to let me breath every once in a while in my own home."

"Momma', exactly what are you doin' to her?"

"The same thing I did with you when I was raisin' you. Keepin' yo' butt in line."

"Military line that is," joked grandma.

"By the way, your father contacted me wanting to know when can he come visit you?"

"To be honest with you momma', I haven't even really thought about sending him a form. Anyway, before long, I'll be a free man in a couple of years. He wasn't lookin' for me too much when I was out there so why start now."

"Because he's your father son! And don't you ever forget it." Grandma' outburst was a surprise to them both, upset over his careless choice of words spoken. He meant no real harm by it. Only that him and his father weren't as close since having been divorced by his mother. "Don't you understand the importance of your father existence? He's the only one you got or will ever have. Nobody is perfect son but blood will ALWAYS be thicker than water. Love your father for what he has done for you and not hold against him for what he hasn't. Many of nights I've cried wishin' for the return of your grandfather and now, all of a sudden, this new generation of disrespectful kids wanna' act like they don't need their parents anymore. Exactly what kind of world are we living in today? Do any of you know?" They both were at a loss for words. "I'm sure we don't," shaking her head in dissatisfaction. "But you wanna' know what's happening now? People are startin' to live a shorter, much lonelier life due to a lack of respect for mankind. The world is at a chaotic state and on my GOD existence, I wish I could save every living soul. Your grandma' doesn't like to see no one struggling or lonely. We can easily make this world a better place if we would just stop with the blatant disgrace towards ourselves and each other. Always love yourself first son and that great ball of fire that shines above us all that we call the sun will be your guide to a healthy, glorious life."

"That was beautiful. I love you momma'."

Ms. Hick reached over to embrace her mother. Nard joined them.

"I love you too grandma. And momma'."

"I know you do child. You see, my two generations of kids with me here today are special. Blessed. Everybody doesn't have what's been embedded in y'all hearts."

"And what's that grandma'?"

"Forgiveness young man. Cause with it, you're both able to move forward in life without holding on to any excess baggage. Free from any unnecessary burden. For those who live to get even, they live to surround themselves in misery and we already know the kind of company those type of people prefer to keep."

"Aint' that the truth momma'. I had this friend in the past who couldn't get over the fact that she was fired from this hospital I used to work at all because she kept being late to work and don't you know every time I went by to check up on her she always kept some sort of liquor bottle beside her. She kept arguing about the years she had worked for that place but she never once took into account how wrong of her it was by not reporting to work on time. What she failed to realize is that they owed her nothing.

If anything, she owed them a big thank you for ever allowing her the opportunity to have worked there in the first place."

"And that's exactly what I'm sayin' to you two right now. You, we, all of us must remember one thing: It's a natural duty to make our world a better place. Oh my lord! Just listen' at me. Mouth runnin' out of control. Y'all tired of hearin' grandma' talk aint' y'all?"

"No mamm. Keep it comin' momma'."

"Not at all grandma'. Like you said before, I am the future but I can't understand what lies ahead without understanding the legacy you left behind for me and momma'. I'm definitely ready to carry that torch."

"I'm sure you are son but like the rose that grew in the concrete jungle, so to shall he or she that thrives to prosper against their oppressor. Are you ready for that challenge son?"

"Only time will tell grandma'. Only time will tell."

CHAPTER 47

"**M**-J! M-J," yelled Kanisha from in his living room. "Don't forget to pack the kids Sponge Bob! You know how much they enjoy playin' with them things!"

"I won't," stating to himself.

The three months of babysitting left him feeling exhausted. Deprived from enjoying any part of a summer vacation while their mothers were away at college. Shenequa contributed very little help reminding him of the duties that came along with being grown before establishing his own domain. His father opposed of her actions and helped out as much as possible, support he really appreciated.

The kids were asleep. He rolled one out in a baby sitter. The other tucked firmly in his arm. Several bags hung from his other shoulder.

"They're go my lil' snukems'," taking hold of the baby in her arms.

"Where's Kandi?'

"She's back at the house with momma'."

"So what are you and the kids plans for today?"

"Oooooh, I don't know. Maybe go swimming. Take a cruise around the world. Who knows."

"Not without payin' for my passport first. It's a jungle out there! And my kids need their protector at their sides at all times."

"M-J! Who's that out there with all that yellin'," yelled Shenequa from her bedroom. The commotion had awoken her out her sleep. She walked into the living room.

"I'm sorry Mrs. Turner. I didn't know you were back there."

"You aiight'. I thought it might've been one of that boy hooligan friends out here. Are you," taking a closer look at her, "Kandi or Kanisha?"

"It's Kanisha mamm."

"And how are you today Kanisha?"

"Just fine Mrs. Turner. I come to relieve your son from his responsibilities for a while before the kids drive him crazy."

Changing diapers all time of the day. Feeding. Burping them. He eventually grew accustom to the routine learning the importance of napping whenever free time permitted itself. Unlike teething, a problem he struggled with the most, came close to driving him crazy. Their cries would turn into a loud shrill making it almost impossible to bare the constant hollering. Now that the babies were getting older those days were starting to be long behind him.

"And how is college?"

"It's going just fine Mrs. Turner."

"Aren't you bout ready to take this hard-headed child of mines with you?"

"Not yet mamm. This his last year of high school and after that, college will be all his."

"And it couldn't have come at a better time. Amen to that. Well, I'll leave you two, or rather four, alone. Bye man-man'. Bye lil-bit'," kissing them both on the forehead.

"How long you plan on keepin' the kids this time?"

"Maybe no longer than several weeks. At least a month."

"Just make sure you be careful with daddy lil' family. Matter fact," kissing her lips, "you be careful with yourself as well."

"Why did you do that? You know I have a boyfriend."

"Hell, kiss him for me too. In fact, tell him I said I love him also."

"Ha, ha, ha. Very funny. Come roll the stroller out to the car for me crazy man."

He knew of her relationship and cared little, if any about it. She hated his wreckless behavior more so than anything but hid a strong feeling towards him that, for some reason, she couldn't seem to shake loose.

Though some nights while away at college, she wondered if he still found her attractive the same way he used to before her pregnancy. His unwanted kiss had answered any possible doubt that might've pondered on her mind in the past.

CHAPTER 48

"**H**ome, sweet home momma."

"And not a minute to soon. My bladder is about to explode."

"What you mean your bladder is about to explode? Momma', what I told you about not mentioning you needing to use the bathroom while out on the highway? I would've easily stopped at one of those convenient stores we passed."

"Chiiiiiild, not in those filthy restrooms. Grandma' to ol' to be catchin' some type of bodily disease from sitting down on one of them filthy toilets."

"Well gone and relieve yourself. I'm about to put something together for us to eat."

"Sounds like a plan to me."

She walked to the bathroom in admiration of her daughter's concern. Her hand struggled with turning the bathroom knob. She squeezed it harder a second time finally getting the door to open. "What's wrong with my hand," stepping inside. A sharp pain rip through her chest causing her to stumble up against the sink for her balance. Her mouth parted to yell for help but failed at uttering a single word. Through all the turmoil, she somehow managed to make it to her bedroom. Lady fur, in a small portrait on the counter, accompanied her resting position on the bed. The thirty-something year old mattresses eased her pain momentarily or so she wanted to believe. Tears started to roll down the crevices of her aging beauty. A sudden appearance of her husband was but a brief glimpse the lower her eyelids rested shut. The beating sound of her heart echoed loud and clear inside her mind as it slowed. Chest pain increasing more. Her hands resting at her side. Lady fur photo was stationed peacefully across her chest.

"MOMMA'! You want collard greens with your neck bones?" She waited on a response. "MOMMA'! YOU HEARD ME! Let me go check on her to make sure the toilet didn't swallow her up." She searched both direction of the hallway. The bathroom door extended outward. Empty. Her mother bedroom door was closed. "Momma', are you in there? Didn't you hear me calling you?" She turned the handle. "Momma', did you hear me calling you?" She neared the bed. "Momma'," shaking her mother body. "MOMMA'! MOMMA! Please answer me!" Her mother remained still. She ran to her bedroom taking hold of the telephone.

"9-1-1. How can I help you?"

"Please, please send me some help to 6030 Nassau Street! My mother isn't moving! She's laid out on her bed!"

"We'll send someone there very shortly mamm."

"Please," her voice trembling worse than before, "please hurry up."

CHAPTER 49

"Let me apologize for placing your visit on hold but mom-dukes and grandma' is subject to pop-up on me any day they feel like it. Just so happen, it was on your day."

"Look, that's your mother and grandmother we're tallkin' about here. Even if it was wifey I would understand. Now anyone other than those three and you might would've received some type of static from me."

"Sort of like what our bodies are feeling right now?"

They remain embraced in each other arms well after her arrival. She wanted this moment to last a life time knowing it was rare he ever held her so strong but yet so gentle in his arms.

"That's long enough Mr. Hick," interrupted a C.O. patrolling the floor.

She swiftly kissed his lips and parted for their seats.

"As always, thank you for coming Peaches. You've been nothing other than good to me and I don't know how I could ever repay you for it."

"Try separating that wedding ring from your finger for me or would you mind me having the honors?"

"I like that. That was cute."

"So what's taking the joke so long to come into fruition?"

He reared back in awe of her millionth attempt.

"I'll say this Peaches, if, and I do mean if, IF we don't make it for some strange reason than yes, I'll be more than honored to make you my future wife. You're dedicated. You've looked out for me at all cost. Had my back through thick and thin. Was there when I needed you the most.

It's easy to say that, in my eyes, you're the total package. Thank you for everything Peaches."

"Yes sir. That's correct. Bernard Hick."

"Let me see," searching for his name over the computer screen. "He's already in a visit mamm. All you have to do is just walk right on in."

"Thank you sir," concealing her concern.

She wondered who possibly could've been visiting him. His family were just there yesterday having left the same day. His brothers paid him a trip earlier this month only to return the following month. There was no one else she could think of. She walked through its entrance taking her time with scanning one side of the room to the other. Her search didn't take long to see what was needed to see.

"Peaches, baby," taking hold of her hand, "you know, one of these days, you're gonna' get ol Nard in a world of trouble."

"But until then sweetie," sliding closer, "you get to have the best of both worlds."

Shontae continued to watch from afar. Their backs faced to her unaware of a third party soon to be joining. At a slow pace, she neared their seats kneeling behind them in awaitance for the right moment.

"Give me a second Peaches. I gotta' go and take a quick leak."

She waited around the time he was at a full stance and leaped over the seat landing him to the ground.

"NEGRO," scratching at his face, "I'M GONNA' KILL YOU!"

The C.O. identified the commotion hurrying in their direction.

"STOP IT MAMM! GET OFF HIM MAMM! Fight in visitation! Fight in visitation," repeated the officer in his walkie-talkie.

CHAPTER 50

Two in the morning. All inmates secured in their cells. Nard lay awoke. Unable to sleep. Refusing to accept the fact that his marriage was possibly over. It took four officers to restrain her clawing hands at his face. The damage wasn't too severe. A slit above the right eye. Several bruises noticeable on the opposite side of his lower face. He talked with her Friday night explaining how she wanted nothing but to rest the entire weekend. Just her and Asia alone at the house. Free from any outside disturbance. Never could he have seen this coming and now that it happened, he wished like hell to turn back the hands of time.

He peered down off the side of his bunk. Red-eyes eyelids rested shut. An MP-3 headset covered his ears. Nard hesitated a moment uncertain if to disturb him this late in the morning.

"Wha pon yo mind bredren?"

"How do you do that," sounding baffled. "How did you know that I was about to say something to you when you never once opened your eyes up to look at me? What are you psychic or something?"

"Jah blesset I wit many grate tings bredren an bein alert pon one surrounding is at de top of dat liss bredren."

"Red-Eyes," laying back on his mat, "I got to be the DUMBEST son-of-a-bitch I know of."

"Wha u mean bredren? No man known to Rastafari is dum. Dem maybe a ballhead. But dem no dum."

"The woman tried to scratch my eyes out earlier today while at visit Red-Eyes."

"Me a notice yu face but wait til yu say sumten bout it to I bredren."

"Wifey celly. She paid me a surprise visit and what a big one it was. My other baby-momma' was already here and after that, all hell broke loose. The woman jumped on me like a tazmanian devil and had no plans of gettin' off me anytime soon."

"Let me tell yu sumtin bredren." He slid off the bunk. Headset placed down on his pillow. "Yu see bredren, a real Rasta-man tek no foolishness from him empress see. Some a dem ack like dem shit no stank. So me, a man bredren, mek dem know up front, 'Look here gal, I de warrior RUN tings! Yu have to mek dem understand dat bredren."

Nard observed as much of his lanky frame the dim room permitted. A silhouette formed from his lengthy dreads swayed slightly pass his waist. His body was devoid of any muscular structure exposed by the wife beater he wore. Harden black skin, scarred by the blistering sun of Kingston, Jamaica at a young age was slightly noticeable.

"I hear you Red-Eyes but dam, it's a lil' too late for all that. Rather I told her in the beginning or not, it's just some things a woman won't tolerate. Especially a married one."

"Den de only grate atvice me have fe give yu bredren is to roll de spliff, dun trip," dancing to his words, "and mek de a ganjay stick, burn up quik. Roll de blunt, don yu front, cause Rasta man no time fo foolish stunts." He handed him a spliff and lighter hidden in his dreads. "Hole dis bredren. Me wan yu smoke til yu choke. Don worry bout me bredren. Enjoy yuself. De ganja will show yu a betta way to resolve tings tomorrow. Don worry bout to day. Live knowen yu do yu bess."

"At a time like this, what's better to have then besides something that'll help ease the mind. Red-Eyes, you never seem to amaze me. Don't forget to place a towel down at the bottom of the door for me. Keep the smell from seeping out the room."

"Bredren," sealing off the door, "wen de smoke hits de air, jus member one ting: De wun who refuses tu dare, remain tu be scared. No fear bredren," pounding his chest. "No fear. Jaaaah!"

CHAPTER 51

S he stormed inside the office feeling fatigued. An entire night spent tossing and turning with lingering images of the damage inflicted on her husband. She called to her job explaining of being about an hour late. The next appointment with her therapist wasn't until December and she refused to wait that long. A patient preoccupied the recliner seat. Shontae politely lifted the older woman up by her small arm and escorted her to the door. "Mrs. Hick! Exactly what are you doing," demanded her therapist. A struggle pursued momentarily before giving in to Shontae's driving force and shoved out the office.

"You better have a very good explanation for your inconsiderate actions! Miss. Livingston has been my most loyal customer since I first started in this profession and out of the blue you just walked right in here forcing her to walk right on out of here. Start explaining yourself Mrs. Hick."

Having a seat on the recliner, "Something serious came up yesterday that couldn't be put on hold until my next visit. Don't you know those people at the prison my daughter father is at tried to imprison me? Can you believe them? The nerves of those people."

"And what exactly would give them the reason for making such a foolish attempt?"

"Well," laying back on the recliner, "there was sort of a minor ordeal that took place."

"How minor Mrs. Hick?"

"Would trying to rip the skin off my husband face be minor enough?"

"Say what! Are you serious Mrs. Hick? What happened?"

"Remember his other quote/unquote 'baby-momma-donna' I told you about in the beginning and how much of a pain AND a problem she was to our marriage?"

"Yes. And?"

"And just so happen yesterday, for the very first time I decided to pay that man a surprise visit, there she was. At visitation. Holding hands with that soon-to-be-ex of mines and at that point, that very moment, is when all hell broke loose except for neither one of them saw it coming until I jumped on him trying to peel back every single piece of flesh that sculptured his handsome face. Some husband he turned out to be."

"Have you thought that maybe you were just jumping the gun a little too soon? They could've been praying. Did you ever even attempt to find out what was really going on? You know, sort of went about it in a rational way."

"You're right. A razor blade would've been much easier then leaving two of my broken nails stuck off in his face."

"No, seriously Mrs. Hick, did you take the time to think for one minute that what you saw was a harmless scenario? She is his son mother you know."

"But she had no right visiting him. I bring his son up with me almost every time our daughter goes to see him. In fact," sitting up, "if I'm not mistaken', he specifically informed me that she will not be placed on his visiting list. Do you see what's going on here? His dirt is only piling up more and more against him."

"But is it that serious enough for you to want to consider him as your ex?"

"I can't tolerate his foolishness any longer. I've done all that I can. Him and that woman have been nothing but problems since day one. Enough is enough. I don't need this sort of drama in my life. I mean, all that I've sacrificed for him and this is how he repay me? With a big slap in the face?" Her hands plastered to her face shielding the pain. "What am I going to do?"

She slid Shontae a box of napkins.

"Lets try and stay focus here Mrs. Hick. True enough, a mistake has been made but it's not the end of the world. Remember what I told you. We are all tested by GOD's obstacles for reason of strengthening. Not weakening. You've overcame much more difficult moments then this."

Wiping her face, "But I love him. And I thought he loved me too. Look how wrong I was."

"This is what I want you to do because I have other clients scheduled in the next few minutes. I want you to try and carry on with a normal day like yesterday never happened. Focus on yourself. Your responsibilities. Your duties at work. Your daughter and anytime those negative thoughts of your husband occur, I want you to first take deep breaths slow and easy several times then count to fifty for me. It's an exercise used for settling down the nerves. I know it's going to be kind of hard in the beginning but just don't give up on it. At all cost, you must remain focus. Your daughter needs her mother more than anything in this world."

"What if your exercise fail? What then?"

"It's failing you right now with your negative thinking. Think positive! Feel blessed and remain living knowing that you're fortunate. Remember, hard times only occur when we fail to make good ones. Now, if you don't mind," lifting Shontae off the recliner, "just be sure the door is fully close on your way out and try and have you a good morning Mrs. Hick."

"Thank you for everything. See you in December."

CHAPTER 52

Frank Scott. Son of a coal miner. Mother of Italian descent. Born in Charleston, West Virginia, watched his father for many nights as a child enter through the front door of their home from a hard day of work. Exhausted. Entire body smeared in black markings. Enough strength for a hot meal, warm shower and the remaining night hours for small talk with his mother before dozing off to sleep. Between the hours of five in the morning to nine, sometimes ten at night, his father could be found somewhere buried beneath the earth surface many miles deep inside of what he called 'The Black Hole'. Angelina Grotti-Scott, whose lineage had ties to Frank Grotti of the mafia family, named her only child in honor of her elder relative. Never has she exchanged any words with him only catching a quick glimpse of his presence at a family reunion in New York City when he wasn't too smothered by relatives or what appeared as mob affiliates shoving him off into the backseat of a limousine. Unfortunately, the wealth of the Grotti family had no immediate ties to any third or fourth cousins excluding her chances at receiving any benefits. She worked part-time as a waitress bringing in extra money spent mostly on her son needs. Luke Scott, the man of the house, disapproved of her working no matter how few of hours the job required. Cooking, cleaning and making sure their son made it back and forth to school as scheduled was all he expected out of her at home. Nothing extra.

Frank grew up a loner. Not by choice but force. The kids in his neighborhood were scarce. Even the houses in the area weren't that many.

Their home swamped by slopes of mountains and large trees blinded him to most of the outside world. His pastime was football. Valuable time he longed to spend enjoying with his father. When asked to join him on his off days which were rare, he awaited for the usual nodding gesture while remaining glued to his favorite love seat staring at game shows on television. Seeming depressed, Frank went up stairs to his room fighting back the tears.

The day was anew. His age much older. He hung around the dinner table. Football twirling around at his fingertips. Angelina standing over the stove preparing supper. His father to walk through the front door at any moment.

"Mom, when is dad goin' to get a better job? You know, one that doesn't take up so much of his time. I can count on one hand the times he ever played with me when I was a kid. One being when I was first born and the other one is when we raced to the mailbox to get out a large check from the state of West Virginia."

"There's nothing wrong with the one your father got now. In case you haven't noticed, he is a fairly big man. He can handle it."

"I'm not disputing that mom but my first sophomore start as a tailback is this weekend which also is our first playoff game and he hasn't seen any of my performance yet. In fact, I can't remember the last time he asked me anything about sports."

"That doesn't necessarily mean he's not concern about what you're doing."

"So he HAS been askin' you about my performance out on the field," expressing with excitement.

"Well...not quite. But he did ask me about your grades."

"MY GRADES! Bullshit mom."

"FRANK SCOTT! We will not be using those words or that tone of voice in this here house."

"What tone of voice? What words are you talkin' about honey?" Luke took a seat at the table. Harden face appearing no different than any other work day except the added wrinkles increasing around his eyes. "What exactly is goin' on in here?"

"Umm, nothing honey," placing a plate down in front of him. "Aint' that right Frank?"

"Yeah mom."

"Your son was just explaining to me how much vulgur language the older kids be using out on the football field honey. That's all."

"Hay dad, I, I mean, we, my football team, got our first playoff game this upcoming Saturday and I was wondering-"

"No," he stated between chewing some food.

"Luke, you didn't even let the boy finish his statement."

Swallowing some water, "I know what it was he was about to say woman and the answer is still no."

"But dad, I make my starting debut and-"

"Boy," leaning closer towards his son. Face squinched tighter. Veins protruding through his forehead. "You really are hard-headed aint' you? You ask me one more damn question about some measly football game and you might not be attending it yourself."

"THIS ISN'T FARE," shoving his chair to the floor.

His father slid back from the table and approached him.

"Son, if you don't pick that dam chair back up and sit your narrow butt down, I'm gonna' take my belt off and whipp you until I discover some coal in your stubborn lil' ass. Do I make myself clear?"

"Luke! Leave the poor child alone," standing between them. "The boy just wants you to attend his game."

"Woman," shoving her out the way, "stay out my business. And as for you, it's clear to me that you've outgrown your britches and this what I want you to do, I want you to go upstairs, to your room, and strip down to your bare skin and I'll be right behind you. You got that?"

He hadn't realized just how close his father stood in front of him. The steaming heat escaping out Luke's nostrils could be felt on his forehead. Their standoff lasted less than a second deciding quickly to bow down and depart knowing he had no win.

"MR. LUKE SCOTT," approaching her husband, "you better not lay one meaty finger on that boy!"

"Woman," pushing her to the ground, "stay your ass there and don't you get up until I tell you to."

It wasn't the first time he laid hands on her. Early on in their marriage he accused her of cheating with a church member where he witnessed the two talking in the parking lot. Without speaking a word, he slapped the man who ran off and then turned to place one of his hand to her throat. Her face a darker red. Eyes bulging out its socket. His grip eased up slightly. "Woman, don't EVER let me catch you in the presence of any man like that again." Nothing later was ever mention about the incident by either of them.

He went into their bedroom closet pulling out a long strip of leather covered in dust particles. The loud, snapping sound it made in the air shook loose anything that clung to it. Frank door was partly ajar. A light breeze greeted his entrance. Curtains dangled at the open window. No sight of his son. A rope tied in a knot at the bottom of a large dresser extended out the window and down side of their two-story home. He ran over towards it viewing outside. "FRAAAAAAAAAAAAANKIEEEEEE EEEEEEEE!"

"HONEY! WOULD YOU ANSWER THAT DOOR FOR ME! I'M STILL IN THE SHOWER!"

"WOMAN, YOU NEED TO HURRY UP AND GET OUT THEN! HELL, I'M BUSY TOO!" The splashing whir of running water ceased. She entered their bedroom. Her body partially wet. A towel wiped dry her breast leaving the other half of her chest exposed. His undivided attention averted from a stack of paperwork on his desk to her nakedness. He waited until she neared grabbing hold of her waist. "You need any help with that young lady?"

She sat down on his lap.

"When I needed your assistance earlier in answering the front door, you refused me. Now that I'm naked and your soldier," squeezing hold of his erection, "is at attention, all of a sudden, your helping hands are all over me."

"What can I say? After twenty-five years of marriage, your beauty hasn't aged a bit. Amazing how married to a federal agent can keep his lady from worrying so much about any bad guys coming to do you harm."

"Not when the baddest of them all is seated underneath my nose."

The doorbell interrupted their cozy moment again. "Dammit honey," springing up out his lap, "I almost forgot someone was at the door! Let me go see who it is."

She threw on a T-shirt and some denims and hurried out their room. The doorbell continued ringing.

"I'M COMING! I'M COMING! Damn! I know I'm a lil' late with answering the door but must they keep pressin' that button until they break it? WHO IS IT," peering through the peephole.

"It's Sam Jones, Sonya. Is your husband home?"

"Sam Jones," reciting his name in her head. "From narcotics task force over ten years ago?"

"That be me Sonya."

Pulling open the door, "Sam Jones! How has it been?"

"Just lovely Sonya. And you?"

"Living with my husband is like surviving in Iraq. On pens and needles with every step."

"I see he aint' changed a bit. I thought by now he would've been gave those ways up."

"His federal job only made matters worse. Come on in Sam. He's back there. HONEY! YOU GOT COMPANY!"

He recognized the man voice making his way into the living room.

"Sweetheart, excuse us for a second."

She watched her husband signal for Sam to follow him outside.

"Well aren't you at least gonna' offer your friend something to eat or drink?"

He stared back at her with a serious look she knew all too well. She headed down the hallway.

"Frank Scott! How's it been pal?"

"What in the hell have I told you about callin' me by my real name? In fact, what in the hell have I told you bout' comin' to my house? Call first and then we'll meet up somewhere later."

"I know Trano but I got some serious trouble that I come to warn you about."

"When have your troubles become mines?"

"When we once confiscated a large amount of money working as partners. Look here man, the Internal Affairs came by my house asking of some specific details about that night but this time he stated he wasn't gonna' stop until some heads fly."

"And your story remained unchanged as the last time right?"

"You know it did Trano. Must I remind you, I come out from under your wings: Tactics Respected And Never Outdated (TRANO)!"

He viewed the entire neighborhood, something his day-to-day life deprived him of lately. School kids wondered about to their bus stop. Parents rushing out their homes seeming late for work. Even the air he breathed seem less congested than usual.

"Just…just stay cool. Can you do that for me? Make no sudden moves."

"Sure thing. But hell, I thought those days were long behind us Trano. That was a lil' over a decade ago. Don't they have some type of time limit in investigating something like that?"

"Not really Sam."

"It don't even matter. Shiiiit', that money is long gone anyway. How bout' you Trano? You enjoyed spending all of yours?"

"I don't know if it's safe to be discussing that out in the open Sam."

"Aaaah Frank, I mean, Trano," detecting the anger in his friend eyes, "aint' nobody but us two out here. It aint' like we just committed the crime yesterday. Stop being so paranoid."

"Just know one thing, Vegas enjoyed me about as much as I enjoyed them."

"Vegas you say? Boy, I'm sure that was a great place to spend all that money at."

"Not all but a nice portion of it. Bills have to remain paid around here if you catch my drift.'

"Trano, buddy, I think I'll be moving on along here. Just wanted to inform you on what to be on the lookout for. Be cool brotha'."

Trano couldn't quite understand why his friend of so many years walked off without sharing their ritual embracement. A firm handshake and hug was practiced upon every greeting and departure of his task force signifying their strength, trust and brotherhood. Maybe the long years apart from one another had changed his former subordinate. He always viewed Sam as the weakest link and wanted only for him to continue professing his innocence just one last time. Maybe the investigation wasn't as serious as it seemed. He dismissed the thought recapturing his wife nakedness laid out on their bed in awaitance of his return. "Here I come honey! Badge, gun, and plenty of fun!"

CHAPTER 53

"You don't think she gone continue refusin' your phone calls forever do you pimpy'," enquired Bruh.

"Being that the incident was only a few days ago, I'm hoping maybe by the end of the week she'll come around."

"And if there's no improvement by then, then what?"

"What else can I do besides nothing? She has every right to cut all ties with me if she so chooses. I was wrong. Dead wrong! Stupid as hell to be exact."

"Don't be so hard on yourself pimpy'. They say real love only strengthens at real times."

"Yeah. For another man probably."

"There you go thinkin' negative again. Lets look at the bright side here, at least you're married to a great woman."

"Past-tense you mean."

"Most men will leave this world without ever having experienced such a blessing."

"Maybe you're right. Maybe I am worrying myself just a lil' too much."

"The best thing for you to do is to maintain a strong relationship with your kids and let the rest try to better itself. She'll eventually come around. Right now, she's just hurt. The wound is a deep cut that'll need time to heal. Remember what you told me, positive progress diffuse negative notions. But take a look at the positive vibe headed in our direction from afar." Nard searched through the crowd of inmates in front of him exiting the recreation area. At first glance it appeared that she was fixated on him alone. "This what I'm gonna' do pimpy', I'm gonna' slide up here to the unit and allow you some private time with her. Holla' back at'cha boy later on. And remember, let it all flow naturally."

Nard veered off in her direction.

"Nice to see you again lieutenant."

"And a good afternoon to you too Mr. Hick. Where you headed?"

"Back to my unit to freshen up. Just finished exercising. Somewhat maintaining my sanity."

"Sounds like a wonderful thing. It's a must that you try and stay focus while you're locked up as much as possible."

"So what's been up with you lately? I haven't seen you in a couple of days."

"You don't have a problem with me taking a few off days do you? By policy, I am obligated to do so."

"You don't hear no type of flak comin' from me. I just wish those days were shared in the comfort of this young man arms somewhere cozy and comfortable."

"And exactly what would you have in mind?"

"For starters," noticing the compound had been cleared of all inmates, "anything your precious heart desire."

"Just that easy."

"I can be your genie but with a million wishes."

"Coming from you, one would be just fine."

He watched her eyes brighten with glee.

"But back to reality being that I'm fortunate enough to have met a new friend, my next objective with it would be to make it last forever."

"How much time you got left Mr. Hick before you are freed?"

"I would say around a year and a half. Maybe less."

"You do realize that I'm not getting any younger here don't you?"

"Judging by your youth, I would say you still have a lifetime of great times left in you."

"Thank you for the compliment young man. You sure know how to make an ol' cougar feel young again. By the way, I'm sorry to hear about your grandmother's death."

"My grandmother's death! What are you talkin' about Ms. Cooper?"

"Saturday evening before I left, your mother called up here asking about how to relay the message to you. I connected her with the chaplain. You mean, they haven't informed you yet? That was over three days ago." He stood motionless. Stunn! Mouth open yet unable to say a word. "Mr. Hick! Are you okay? Would you like to sit down in my office? Say something?"

His blank expression unchanged. She signaled of him to follow. They made it inside.

"Ms. Cooper?"

"Please, call me Stacy."

"Stacy, I…"

"Take your time Mr. Hick."

"I…I just can't believe this is happening. My closest friend. Gone! And I wasn't even around to tell her I love her. DAMN," pounding a fist atop of her desk.

Barging through the door, "Is everything alright in here lieutenant?"

"I'm fine Mr. Dixon. Thank you. He was just venting his frustration out. A death in the family." The officer stepped back out. "Will you be okay Mr. Hick?"

"I have no other choice but to. She wouldn't want it any other way. Man, I still can't believe she's gone like that. Now that's gonna' be one hard pill to swallow."

"If you need me for anything, I mean anything, don't hesitate for one second to come talk to me."

"Thank you Stacey. And in the near future, it's aiight' for you to call me Nard."

"Alright then Nard," she smiled. "You do know that you're authorized to make a phone call over to the chaplain to contact your family. It's up to you."

"Nah'. I'm cool. I think I'll go back to my cell and relax a lil'. Take it easy."

"You sure you're going to be okay?"

Walking over towards the door, "Maybe…maybe not."

There was really nothing she could do. A comforting hug, she was sure, would've eased some of his hurt but was against everything her job description stood for. Though one day, soon, she knew that wish would come true. For now, she could only keep him in her prayers and under close surveillance.

"Hello, momma?"

"Hello son. How you holding up?"

"Under the circumstances, I'm makin' it. What about you? You aiight'?"

"Well…I'm livin'. One day at a time. It's only difficult for me to deal with when ever I'm not active with something around the house and know soon as I stop with whatever I'm doin', THAT'S when I become sadden."

"Hang in there momma'. We gonna' be aiight'. What about your other two boys?"

"The usual. One too lazy to make any improvements while the other can't excel beyond a nine-to-five."

"Don't you know I just got word of grandma's death about an hour ago?"

"Are you kidden' me! That was late Saturday evening when I called up there. Not to long after they informed me she was gone at the hospital."

"Momma', these people around here don't take nothing serious except writing infractions or sending someone to the shu. So what happened?"

"Son," building the strength to explain herself, "she went and used the bathroom while I prepared dinner. When I yelled for a reply, I got none. That's when I went in search of her and noticed she wasn't in there. Her bedroom door was closed so I walked over to open it. She lay resting on her bed. I walked over and shook her body several times but she still wouldn't respond. The only option I had left was to call 911 and now, a few days later, my tears has been my closest friend."

"Well, you're definitely not alone momma'. So don't ever think that for one minute."

"Thank you son but it's like momma' said to us both during visitation, we only have one mother and one father and lord KNOWS she's gonna' be missed dearly. You mind changing up the topic a lil' cause the more we discuss it the more I become nauseated."

"To add more difficulty to our problem, Shontae caught Peaches up here visiting me on Sunday."

"Say what! Are you serious! Say it aint' so!"

"We wasn't doin' nuthin' but just sittin down having a conversation. Surprise visit on Shontae's part."

"Surprise or not, you know how much that girl hate Peaches."

"Tell me about it. Anyway, she won't accept none of my calls. I can't even get in contact with my daughter."

"You got no one to blame but yourself. Even if she decides to leave you. Why would you put that girl on your list knowing how much she dislikes Peaches?"

"I don't know momma'. Silly me. I thought I could keep the two separated on visiting days."

"That girl was breaking her neck to come see you. Almost every weekend she was up there. Even bringing your son with them all the time. If you ask me, but only because I'm your mother, I would say you deserve to be alone. Maybe then you'll understand the importance of respecting the most precious gift god will ever bless man with in this cold world."

"Maybe you're right. Maybe I have been foolin' myself all this time. It probably is meant for me to be a single man til' I die."

"Boy, you sound like a dam fool! Where is your head at? You know what I think your problem is, you keep thinkin' life is a game. Let me say this to you cause I'm gettin' disgusted just thinking about it. Learn to love yourself FIRST before loving another. If you can figure that out, you just figured out the true meaning of life. I love you. Have a nice day and oh yeah, grow up son…please. Bye-bye."

CHAPTER 54

"**C**ome on child! Snap," snapping her fingers in front of Shontae's face, "out of it! You been in that daze of yours for way to long now. That's how people go crazy girl! I know he's your sweetheart and everything but there's no need of worrying yourself senseless over spilt milk. His lost, his cost. Tax his ass for it! Make him understand that any mistake made out of ignorance is expensive."

"This is not some kind of budget cut I'm dealing with here. He's my husband. As well as my friend. Someone I thought I could confide in but now it's all a dream."

"And a real one at that. Look here woman, you got it going on! What man wouldn't want to make you his wife. I mean, I'm sorry that your Romeo forgot how to serenade his main lady but there's Leonardo, Captain Jack Sparrow, hell, there's even a handsome Shrek out there somewhere. In other words, your choice for a better man is very broad. Use your playing field to your advantage."

"Mrs. Hick! Would you mind reporting to my office please. Thank you."

"See what I mean. And that man is rich. Get up and go see just how much he really needs you."

"Why me god," staring up at the ceiling.

"Cause you're still the chosen one. Now, get, get, get," lifting Shontae up by the arm.

"Some friend you are."

He waited at the door.

"Good afternoon Mrs. Hick. Please, come on in. I noticed you not to long ago returning from your lunch break. Did you enjoy yourself cause if not, I'm soon to be leaving for mines and your welcome to join me if you like."

"Thank you for the invite but I'm sort of watching my weight."

"Didn't hurt to try," he smiled. "Please, have a seat. My true reason for calling you into my office is because I've sort of noticed these past two days a lack of pep in your step. Even your face lacks that usual gloat about itself. Now, with me being the concern boss that I am, without any strings attached, it's only right of me to ask you if everything alright?"

"Not really sir but I'll be okay. Just something only time can heal."

"And a good friend also. I've told you once before that if there's ever any problems with you, no matter how serious, to contact me. I know a lot of big people in a lot of big places who knows how to turn a frown upside down."

"You think they know how to grant me a new life?"

"It can't be that bad Mrs. Hick. Judging by what I've witnessed and slightly experienced in the past, you're one tough customer. I just hate that your husband caught on to your true worth by embracing you forever."

"Try tellin' him that."

"Would you mind then if I call him at prison and inform him," he joshed grabbing hold of his phone. "You know I can."

"That won't be necessary Mr. Smith. I think he's getting the message."

"Hard times at home?"

"Very."

"Well, you know being married to a prisoner has its serious ups and downs. A lot of space between you two to deal with. No more private time together for those private moments. The worst one is those long, cold lonely nights. Like I said, your husband doesn't realize just how blessed he really is."

"He will once he receive those divorce papers."

"You can't be serious Mrs. Hick? How much harm can an imprison man actually cause?"

"Enough to where he can't be trusted anymore."

"Care to explain?"

"I don't think it's a good time."

"Maybe you're right. But you didn't tell me no and that's a good sign coming from you. So this what I need for you to do, at your earliest convenience, get in touch with me and I'll allow you to relieve that pain or stress of yours you got built up inside you over at a friendly place of eatery. Your choice. A deal," extending a hand across his desk. She watched it linger in the air deciding no harm could be caused by shaking it. His grip was firm and gentle. Her body weakened at his touch. The feeling started to remind her how much she was missing the comfort of a man at home. She hadn't realized the lengthy time her hand remained held to his as they stood to their feet. "And remember what I told you, just one call is all it takes and I'll come running," releasing her hand.

She turned to walk out knowing a terrible mistake had been made. The love for her husband was still strong. Even after their horrible dilemma. But enough was enough. The unnecessary drama in her life had become too much and she knew of only one way with resolving it.

CHAPTER 55

"Yo bredren, fo de secun time in tree days, me notice yu mopen roun again. Yu know wha me tink wrung wit yu bredren, yu no get nuff herbs in yu life. Yu live wit de original don dada, bredren. Yu know how me'a get down. Like we say in Jamaica, 'COME DOWN SELECTA', fo enty-ting yu need. Rememba, we'a bredrens. I and I."

"I feel you Red-Eyes. Thanks. I got some bad news earlier today. My grandmother passed away this past Saturday."

"Me sorry to hear dat bredren. Moment of silence fo we luv ones no here enty mo." They bowed for a brief second. "Nuff blessen pon dose who once shared de same space wit us. May Jah continue to allow dere existence to live in de hearts...JAAAH...RASTAFARI!"

"Preciate' that Red-Eyes. And still, I'm amazed by your many talents."

"Bredren, life'a much mo den a circus anna clown. Jus know me tek no part in non a dem."

"She will be missed dearly. One of the realist soldier of her time."

"She pass dat on tu granson bredren. Me notice de tru general in yu. Unnerstan one ting bredren, me mingle mongst no ballhead nor edeots. Defnately no bahty bwoy. Wen yu first move in dis cell, me give yu twenty-for howas to watch an see if yu conduct yuself inna orterly fashion. Yu pass de tess in less den dat by not tuchin a ting wen yu first cum in de cell awaiten me return frum de rec yard and de sweetest one a'dem is dat yu no snore. After dat bredren, we'a flowed like a tru Rastah perfomen at a jam fess. Yu cool wit me bredren. Me got yu back. Fo enty'ting bredren. Enty'ting!"

"I appreciate that Red-Eyes," their hands clasped together. "If it's aiight with you celly, I'd like a lil' private time alone for a moment. Somewhat clear my head of a few things."

Red-eyes respected the request. Nard fought back the tears long enough before feeling it streak along both sides of his face. Trouble at home, incarceration, his grandmother death, all caused him to question himself as to when will the pain end. Being alive made him realize one thing: "God awaketh! Then God testeth!"

CHAPTER 56

"If it aint' the one, the only, Mr. Mike Senior. Long time no see ol' friend. So tell me, what honor do I have to be blessed by your presence on this Saturday weekend amongst a house of failures, flunkies and fags?"

"After gettin' a whiff of the mess your name been brewin' in lately, I figured the least I could do was come pay my partna' a visit and find out from the horses mouth on what's REALLY goin' on at your home and sir, shit aint' lookin' to pretty back in the city."

"Nah' Mike, it's not. Once again, the other man tucked away in my pants got me into something even God couldn't fix."

"That serious?"

"More serious than it should be. I mean, true enough, I was wrong for allowing Peaches to visit me but she's family. Not by marriage but carriage. She had my first child. Don't that at least count for something?"

"Try askin' wifey that and watch and see how fast she try rippin' your head off your shoulders."

"I had the slightest of clue she was gonna' pop up like that. A couple nights ago before she came, she said that her and Asia was gonna' stay home and chill. Before I knew anything, she crept up on our seats so fast that by the time I turned around after standing up, it felt like Hurricane Katrina had rushed through the building. I stayed pent to the ground for about five minutes before they were able to pull her off me. See the scar above my eye."

"And the one on side of your face too. Judging by your war-wounds, it clearly looks to me that you're back at your ol' tricks again. Still playin' the games you used to play so well. I thought that lifestyle was ol' news? As in, played out? What happened?"

"Like I said earlier, she came up unannounced and received the biggest surprise of her life."

"But that's one that never should've been gift wrapped in the first place. You knew that shit was wrong. Dead wrong! Now you probably done lost the best thing to ever happen to you. A got-damn shame. When are we really gonna' step our game up Nard? I mean, what is it really gonna' take?"

"I couldn't even begin to tell you Mike. Maybe my life is just one big gimmick after all. A fluke."

"I wouldn't say that homeboy but I will say this, at the rate you're goin', start preparing yourself for the coldest winter ever cause that's exactly the kind of lonely road your setting yourself up for."

"Is that your only reason for coming up here to see me? Just so you can chew me out?"

"Not at all my friend. My mission is different. I come to see for myself just how much pain you're actually in and to me, it seems like a lot. When was the last time you spoke to her?"

"I haven't."

"That's not good at all. This what I can do, I'll somehow, accidentally, bump into her in traffic somewhere. In fact, as soon as I make it back to the city, I'll pay her a visit. It's been about a month anyway since the last time I checked up on her and Asia. Hopefully she'll give me a minute or two of her time after the mess you made. Long enough to determine exactly just how strong the hate outweighs the love for you but in the meantime, let her be. She'll need some valuable time to heal without you bothering her. Women can be very evil when we play with their hearts. Your mistake was critical."

"Mike...thank you man. That woman means everything to me."

"I know she does...PLAYA," shaking his head. "Just finish ridin' the remainder of your months out and before you know it, you and that ol' lady of yours will be back in the sack."

"I hope you right Mike."

"By the way, your grandmother funeral was beautiful."

"I'm sure it was homeboy," gazing off into space, "I'm sure it was."

Mike arrived back at the city shortly after sunset. Almost every light appeared to be on throughout Nard's house. A good sign. Asia answered the knock at the door.

"Haaaay' uncle Mike!"

"Haaay' Asia," reaching down for a hug.

"Uncle Mike," placing one hand on her hip while pointing with the other, "you still owe me a trip to Chuk-E-Cheese!"

"I know I do Asia and I apologize. I haven't forgotten' about you. Uncle Mike is saving up every single penny so when we finally get there, you can eat up every slice of pizza your precious lil' heart desire."

"That sounds like a plan to me uncle Mike."

"ASIA! WHO IS THAT AT THE DOOR YOU'RE TALKEN' TO!"

"UNCLE MIKE MOMMY!"

"INVITE HIM IN!"

"Mommy said for you to come in uncle Mike."

"Thank you Asia."

Strolling into her living room, "Alright Asia, it's time for you to be getting ready for bed."

"Aaaaaah mommy. Do I have to?"

"What is your age young lady?"

"A big-girl eight."

"Which means your big-girl self has to abide by big-mommy rules. I'll be in their shortly to tuck you into bed."

"Alright mommy. You win this time. But one day," making her way towards her room, "one day I'll have my way and I'll be telling YOU what to do!"

"Wonderful kid aint' she," stated Mike.

"Plenty of laughs."

"How you been Shontae?"

"Mike, before you say anything, I already know why you're here. Soo don't even waste your time."

"You know how fast words travel Shontae."

"Well, relay this message back to your friend…the divorce papers are en route to his location. I hope he enjoys what he asked for."

"Woooooooow! And without a second thought."

"Just that easy Mike. It's over. I don't deserve it nor do I have time for it."

"Seeing that I'm a minute to late as far as bringing it all to some kind of understanding, at least no one can't say I didn't try to reconcile y'all differences cause I did. Who knows, in the future, anything is possible. Even you having a change of heart."

"I've enjoyed your company Mike but," opening the front door, "have a good night."

"Like I said," approaching the door, "I tried."

"Your friend will be aiight'. He's a big boy. At least he think he is. Good night Mike."

He lingered outside the door displeased with the outcome. Her decision was finalized. There was nothing he could do but hope she was kidding about the divorce papers though he doubt that seriously.

"You have a collect call from…Bernard Hick'. If you accept the call, please press 1."

"What's up Nard?"

"You made it back in one piece didn't you?"

"Without a doubt. I not to long ago left from over your castle."

"And, how did it go?"

"Oh, it's bad. Real bad. The woman said for you to kill yourself."

"Tell me your bullshittin'?"

"Not really but the hate towards you is strong. But possibly not definite."

"That's a good thing then right?"

"For you, maybe. But still, don't bother her. Not just yet."

"But I miss my boo! I catch hell with these cold walls I'm surrounded by with keeping myself warm."

"What about Sam Susie?"

"Very, very funny sir."

"Anyway, play your cards right and remember, keep it tight. Capishe?"

"See senior, see. I'm out."

CHAPTER 57

She stood outside the Condominium Castle Hotel unfazed by the crashing sound of thunder and lightning. The trench coat she wore was drenched in rain. Her hair soaked as well. The last thing she concerned herself with was her appearance and wanted the occasion to be over with as soon as possible. Occupants inside the lobby watched on as her drunken stature staggered toward the elevator. The doors slid open and quickly closed after her entrance. She searched around. No one aboard. She stared at the twenty-two numbers that lit up on the inside pressing the number thirteen. The door slid open seconds later. A long corridor extended out in front of her with doors to the left and right. She stepped out in search of room 20.

"Yes Stacey. First thing Monday morning we'll go over all the paperwork in my office. Some of the numbers aren't adding up correctly somewhere and the last thing we need is for an auditor to accuse us of cooking the books. Enron went down in history for that shit. Not us."

"KNOCK-KNOCK-KNOCK!"

"What the," peering at the time on his watch. "Stacey, look here, someone is at my door. I'll talk to you later. Enjoy your weekend." He wasn't expecting any company this late in the evening and slid into his robe. "WHO IS IT?" No one responded. He opened the door. "Mrs. Hick! My god! You're a mess! Come in, come in. Is everything alright?"

Her trench coat fell to the floor. His eyes widen. The sight of her nakedness was one he could've adored for a lifetime. She stepped inside encircling his body completely with hers.

CHAPTER 58

Shontae stumbled through the front door of her home in rush of the bathroom. Vomit just seconds away from spewing out her mouth. The alcohol she consumed earlier unsettled her stomach along with the horrendous act she indulged in.

"Mrs. Hick, are you okay," questioned the babysitter standing outside the bathroom.

The puking sound soon ceased. Her head remain lowered as she motioned for her to leave. She wanted no parts of any questioning and preferred to be alone in her misery. The room started spinning as she stood to her feet. She could still taste the alcohol inside her mouth and rinsed it out with some mouthwash. A dim view of her bed displayed relief. "What have I done," falling out over the king size mattresses. Her therapist was probably right. What she saw involving Nard and Peaches could've been just socializing. No strings attached. Jumping the gun might've been wrong of her but more wrong of him for lying to her about excluding his baby-mother from visiting him. She lay confused. Hurt. Uncertain of her tomorrow. Contemplating rather two wrongs were justifiable. The pain she felt in her heart was deep. She rested over on her side. Her pillow wet from tears. No one could ever know of her rendezvous. Not a single soul. A secret she would leave this earth with buried beneath its darken soil. If word ever seeped out on his end, she would just have to deny it. It wasn't too long before loud snoring echoed throughout the room.

CHAPTER 59

"**M**r. Trano?"

Pressing down the speaker button on the phone, "Yes Claire."

"There's two gentlemens at my desk requesting to speak with you sir. Shall I send them in?"

"Sure. Why not."

Turning to face them, "His office is straight down the hallway. Third door on your left."

"Much ablige mamm."

Trano sat calmly at his desk awaiting for their knock.

"Come in gentlemens!"

"Mr. Frank Scott, aka, Trano?"

"Yes sir. That would be me. How can I help you?"

"Good afternoon sir. My name is Mr. Smalls and this here is my associate, Mr. Biggs," nodding his head at Trano, "and we're with the Internal Affairs."

"I've been expecting you."

"In that case sir, you wouldn't mind me having a seat then would you?" Trano pointed at a chair in front of his desk. "Sir, what I'm about to play to you is evidence linking you to the involvement of $50,000's stolen out of a confiscation room you had access to on your shift the night it came up missing."

"Must you gentlemens be wasting my time. Shouldn't you guys be back at your desks planning for your pension?"

Mr. Small's pulled out a phone from within his jacket and toucched its screen.

"Please Mr. Trano, listin' to this recording sir:

> "When have your troubles become mines?"
> "When we once confiscated a large amount of money working as partners. Look here man, the I.A. came by my house asking of some specific details about that night but this time he stated he wasn't gonna' stop until some heads flop."
> "And your story remain unchanged as the last time right?"
> "You know it did Trano. Must I remind you, I come out from under your wings: Tactics Respected And Never Outdated!"

He pressed stop signaling for his co-worker to step out the room.

"That coward son-of-a-bitch! So you got me on tape. Big fuckn' deal."

"I'm sure it's nothing of concern to you Mr...Trano." Mr. Biggs returned in the company of two federal agents. "Mr. Trano, I think it's time we go for a ride."

The agents grabbed hold of his arms escorting him out the office.

"Wait a minute. WAIT A MINUTE," snatching loose their hold. He looked everyone in their eyes. "Before the sun goes down, I'll be out. Free! Hopefully lockin' up your sons' and daughters' one day. So be sure to tell they lil' bad asses to be on the lookout"

"Get his big mouth ass out of here," instructed Mr. Smalls.

CHAPTER 60

"**B**ERNARD HICK!

His eyes awoke but didn't move. He waited to hear his name call again. Not a word. Red-Eyes entered the cell.

"Yo bredren, yu no hear dem?"

"Hear what celly? I was sleep."

"DIS," handing him an envelope. "De C.O. call yu twice."

"For a minute, I thought I was dreamin' when I heard my name. I waited for him to say it again but I aint' hear nuthin'."

"No bredren. Dis, dis real," handing him the mail.

"Give thanks bredren."

"Enty' tyme bredren. Me got oter tings tu ten tu bredren. Cee yu tunite."

He studied the name on the envelope.

"Bout' time you holla' at'cha boy," ripping it open.

Dear Nard,

How have you been? Let me first apologize for my absence lately but as we are both aware, things have changed. DRAMATICALLY! By the way, Asia is fine and said to tell you 'hi' and that she loves you. Now, for my main purpose in writing you is clearly attached to this letter.

He slid her letter to the side and pulled out more papers from within the envelope. The heading, in bold print, stated: FILING FOR DIVORCE IN THE SUPERIOR COURT OF MUSCOGEE COUNTY DIVISION!

That's right! Divorce papers. To make a long story short, please sign the papers at your earliest convenience. You would be doing both of us a big favor. And one more thing, please…don't call me ever again.

The papers slid from out his hand and onto the floor. Heart right behind it. He took full blame. She had every right to move on with her life. He picked the papers up off the floor and started reading them again. He folded them back into the envelope and placed it on his bunk.

He walked out into the day room and sat at a table. Alone. In hopes of no one disturbing him. Her laughter caught his attention over the commotion. Ms. Cooper and the C.O. was both heading out the unit.

"MS. COOPER," rushing to catch up. She looked back and stopped.

"Hello there Mr. Hick! Will you please excuse us Mr. Jones."

"Yes mam, lieutenant. I'll talk with you later. Be sure to give me a call before you clock-out tonight."

"Will do. And how are you Mr. Nard?"

"I'm koolen'."

"Oh, is that so? You don't appear to be. You look sort of, down. Where's that natural gloat of yours I'm used to seeing?"

"Hidden behind the pain my soon-to-be ex wife just caused."

"Oh wow! And how so?"

"I got some divorce papers in the mail today."

"That's not good at all. Are you sure that's what she wants? Maybe she's bluffing."

"I doubt that. She's one that's not only serious but DEAD serious."

"Well, do you plan on signing them?"

"I guess. What else can I do? Hope it's some type of joke she's playin'? The papers seem real to me."

"You know your wife better than I do."

"First of all, before I do anything, I gotta' make me some copies to have for myself but I don't have a copy card. And the copy machine in education is broke."

"There's a copy machine in the back."

"The one between these two units?"

"Of course. Where elese?"

"They'll let you do that for me?"

"At 6P.M., they better be off work and done left a couple of hours ago."

"I really would appreciate that Stacey."

"I can't tell! Why you still standing there."

He went to get the envelope. She stood in the same spot when he returned.

"I'm ready."

She led him through one of the locked doors that separated the two housing units. The secretary office was empty. They stepped inside.

"Gone and make as many copies as you need and make it fast. I'm already in violation for having you back here like this in the first place."

He pressed several buttons on the printing machine.

"What's up with this thing? Every time I press copy, it always says legal or mailing size."

"Move out the way boy. It always gotta' be a woman doing a mans job."

She squeezed between him and the machine. He wanted to pull her closer to him but remained cautious.

"You see how easy that was," peering over her shoulder at him. "All you had to do was-"

His lips met hers. She felt surprised but enjoyed it.

Pulling herself loose, "This isn't right. I mean, right here?"

"Are you afraid?"

She stared in his bold eyes and started to unfasten her uniform. She knelt down on both hands and knees and placed herself in a doggy-style position.

"Do what you want baby but please," angling her face around at his, "be gentle."

He quickly undressed and positioned himself behind her. His finger gently slid within her noticing its moistness. Deciding not to indulge further with foreplay, he began to penetrate her with caution. She relaxed her entire body felling him fill her inside completely. His hands were gripped tight to her waist while gently rocking her back and forth. "That feels soooo good Nard," she mentioned softly. He noticed her weaken' in the hips and held her in place. Cum oozed down her inner thighs. Her ecstasy reaching its peak. His implosion within her triggered an eruption in return.

"Compound to lieutenant, over."

"Oh shit!" She clamber to her feet. "Go'head compound."

"We got a problem down in special housing. Will need your assistance, over."

"Ten-four. Be there in one minute."

"You're perfect. Did you know that?"

"And you fit well but sorry," hurrying her clothes back on, "we have to go."

"Maybe our next place of rendezvous will be much longer."

"Hopefully somewhere in the free world."

"Oh, most definitely." He walked with her to the unit exit. "See you tomorrow?"

Whispering in his ear, "Have a great night."

CHAPTER 61

"**Y**o' M-J, where you at in your house right now?"

"Fixin' me some grubbs big boy. What's up?"

"Hurry up and get to your computer. Fast!"

"What's so damn important that you want me to stop what I'm doin' and put down this big, juicy nanna-fish dish on whole wheat bread I'm a second from biting into?"

"This some important shit you need to see. Have you made it there yet?"

"Yeah, yeah! I'm right in front of it."

"Check this out, I was browsing around on it shortly ago. You know, updating myself with the freakiest of freaks indulging in a three-way when this UNBELIEVABLE scene popped up out of know where on the screen. Click on to www.icantbelieveitsnotsex.com. Then, go to 'for your eyes only' and tell me if I'm dreaming or if seeing IS believing because if that's not my homeboy and his new-found family humpin' around then, Bobby Brown should've just remained underground where crack is more accepted."

M-J finished typing in the information awaiting for it to appear across the scene.

"WHAT THE! THAT FAGGOT MUDDA-FUCKA'! I bought it back! How this shit happin'?"

"Somewhere between you sellin' and buyin' it back from him. Oh Boy-George went and made a power move on you playa'. Without your consent!"

202

"J-B, we gotta' get this off the internet."

"I'm with you on that but how? Where to start?"

"By going back to the porno shop."

"I'll be there in twenty minutes."

They pulled into the parking lot. Trash thrown across the ground. The lawn lacked any maintainence in months. Two-by-fours were nailed to the windows and entrance door.

"Aint' this some shit! This place done closed down! Now how am I suppose to get in touch with this dude? My ass might be in some deep shit now. It got to be someone on the internet I can contact and have them remove it. I'm sure I'll get charged like hell to have it done but right now, that don't even matter."

"Besides, what's the chances of them girls lookin' on the internet for the website? They aint' on that type of time I know."

"You might be right. I might be panicking for nothing. Maybe I'll," their dialogue interrupted by the sound of his phone ringing. "Yeah, who this? KANISHA! Wha-what's wrong! Why you yellin'? Where you at? I'll be there in a minute."

"What's up playa'? Something wrong?"

"I'm dead. Dead and stankin'."

CHAPTER 62

Months had gone by. Still, no visits. No letters. Nard's mother brought his son and daughter to see him every so often. Not as much as Shontae used to but it did help ease his troubles about their well-being. He held on to the divorce papers for several months waiting for a possible change of heart from her. It never happened. As requested, he mailed it back off to her without any pleading on his part.

His affair with Ms. Cooper kept his mind preoccupied for the most part. Once during the afternoon meal, she walked beside him the entire time through the serving line up until he grabbed his tray. He hadn't noticed just how careless they were for unknowing what staff member present at the time might've had them under close surveillance. Nard confronted her about it during their rendezvous. She grew offensive.

"So now you're afraid to be seen with me in public?"

"Woman, are you insane? I'm in prison! You're not! I don't want to see you lose your job because of our carelessness. We just gotta' be more on point. That's all."

After an apology, she knelt down in front of him in a secluded area and performed oral sex.

Nard hung out on the recreation yard exercising. The pull-ups had started to form his upper body in a more defined, muscular shape. He admired the results in his cell mirror whenever his shirt was off. Big-Bruh' came running from around the corner in flashing what appeared like a sheet of paper.

"PIMPY'! PIMPY'!" Nard dropped down off the pull-up bar. "Damn pimpy'! I'm surprise to still see you out here this late in the evening. But guess what? You won't BELIEVE what I just got!"

"Another love letter from baby-momma'."

"Yeah', right. But seriously?"

"How bout' a-"

"RELEASE PAPERS," shoving it in Nard's hand.

"That's great Bruh'!"

"Can you believe it? I'm finally going home! This calls for a drink."

"Say what," lifting his head up from reviewing the paper.

"Just kidden' pimpy'. I got the paperwork from my case manager about an hour ago. I leave tomorrow."

Tomorrow? As much as Nard was excited for his friend, he found it hard accepting the fact that he would be on the compound without his closest associate around.

"Are you ready?"

"HELL YEAH I'm ready! I've been waiting on this for a long time. Thanks to the change in the new crack law goin' retroactive, it's over. Fanito!"

"Look here, you already got my mother's number and address. Plus my information. Be sure you stay in contact with me. Aiight' big-fella'?"

"I got you pimpy'." They embraced for a brief second. "Take care yourself Nard."

"You do the same Bruh'. And don't be out there drinkin' either. Your daughter needs her father more so than ever. Stay focused at all times."

"Yeah', you're right. Let me go and get back to the unit. I got a few important phone calls to make."

Nard watched him stop in his tracks, turned around and stood there.

"Thank you for everything pimpy'. I owe you big, big homie."

He saluted Nard and vanished off behind a building.

CHAPTER 63

"**H**OW DARE YOU! HOW DARE YOU STOOP SO FUKEN' LOW LIKE THAT!"

"Kanisha! Let me ex-"

"SHUT UP! Shut your ass up Mike! As long as I or the kids are alive, don't you EVER look for us again a day in your life! I'm going straight down to the police precinct and put a restraining order on your ass for as long as you live!"

"Kani-"

"SHUT UP," throwing her keys at him. She picked up a lamp in his living room just seconds from tossing it before Shenequa walked through the door intercepting her throw.

"Hold on child! Now, I understand my son might deserve it but not with this," placing it back down. "I got a Louisville slugger in my closet. You need me to go get it?"

"Yes! TWO of them if you got it!"

"Momma', this woman done gone crazy."

"Not yet! But I'm about to!"

She charged him. Shenequa withheld her back.

"What's goin' on in here? Will somebody tell me what's the problem?"

"Tell her Mike Junior! Tell her with yo' sleezy ass!"

"Momma', I will but later. But first, get her out of here. The woman tryin' to kill me."

"She might need to. Young lady, I'm sure you have a great explanation for your reason of battery but there's no sense in gettin' yourself in any trouble behind it. So just calm down, have a seat, and lets get to the bottom of things."

"There's no way in hell I'm ever sitting down in the same room with this-this...ASSHOLE!"

"Aiight' young lady. Enough is enough. That, he might be but there's only one person who's authorized to refer to him as such in this house. I think I'm gonna' have to ask you to leave."

"Fine with me," picking her keys up off the floor. "Mike, I meant every single word of what I said. Don't ever call us and don't even THINK about comin' around us. EVER!"

The door slam. A glass photo on the wall fell to the floor.

"What exactly have you went and done to that woman this time?"

"Momma', my dear sweet mother."

"That I am but I don't believe that's going to save you. Go ahead, finish up."

"The internet, me and my family tree. Exposed to the entire world."

"You and your family are on the internet? And how is that a bad thing? You have a nice family."

"DID, did have a nice family. Now it's mayheim and hopefully not a murder."

"BOY, will you just come on out and say it! I got things to do, hell."

"Not only was our first encounter one for the history books but it was also history accidentally exposed to the public. Sexual exposure."

"Boy, I'm tired of playinn' riddles with you."

"I put the event that you caught us in on DVD and somehow it accidentally got into the wrong hands."

"Yeah, YOURS! I'll be a donkey's ass! Know wonder she tasted blood. But I aint' surprise. Nope. Not one bit. I just hope you haven't been snoopen' around here recording me and your father or their WILL be a murder charge around here today."

"When you kicked me out the house, my money had run out. So I went and sold it to a porn shop for $5000's but when I got word about their pregnancy, the money had already been mostly spent and that's when I sold my car to go and buy it back."

"How could you have been so stupid son? In fact, don't even answer that. Don't you know they could've made a copy of the disc and then sold you back the original one without you ever knowing it until it's too late such as now?"

"You're right momma'."

"It's obvious it doesn't do any good to punish you because this lesson learned will probably punish you for the rest of your life. I just hope you can continue to live with yourself and not try to go out the easy way by committing suicide."

"Not an option momma'. Things will be back to normal before we know it."

"And Jesus parting the Red Sea is gone drown in between. I'm through discussing this. Momma' is goin' to rest her nerves. I suggest you do the same."

"Nah'. I think I'm gonna' take me a walk."

"And son...don't come back."

CHAPTER 64

The envelope remained on her night stand next to her bed day-in and day-out. Unharmed. Untouched. Many nights she lay. Staring. Too afraid to review the contents inside. In her mind, she wanted their relationship terminated. Her heart opposed which left her stuck between a rock and a hard place. She admired him for his great qualities as a man and devoted love towards his family. If it hadn't been for his son baby-mother, she would've considered their marriage to be the perfect dream. Peaches! The one thing that fueled her anger the most. She sacrificed more than enough by accepting the fact that Peaches would be around forever but couldn't tolerate her being anywhere near Nard. The exact same affliction she would continue to face if she decided to stay in their marriage and now that he returned the letter, she regret having sent it off for fear of him having signed it.

The sexual encounter with her boss was a huge mistake. She found him hanging more and more around her cubicle consulting with her friend. A verbal altercation between them soon pursued one afternoon. Slanderous words were exchanged by her followed with a, "I QUIT!" She ended up finding employment as a legal assistant.

The entire house was pitch black. Asia asleep. She walked into her bedroom. Tired but not sleepy. Catching up on some late night reading seemed the best remedy until she dozed off. She flicked on the lamp. Their it remained underneath it. Unharmed. Untouched. She searched the drawer for a novel titled, "Mist Beneath The Sheets," and couldn't keep her eyes off his handwriting. Several chapters were read and placed the book beside her. She sat up against the head board. The envelope snatched off the night stand. "Why are you making this so hard for me?" She ripped it open, pulled out the papers and shredded it into small pieces hurling it to the floor. "THERE! YOU HAPPY NOW! You won my heart," crying herself to sleep.

CHAPTER 65

"**W**ell momma', this is it. That day has finally arrived."

"Yeah' son and I'm proud of you."

"Did you expect anything less?"

"Out of you, I would have to say fifty-fifty. Me actually knowing who you are, your mind has a tendency of comin' and goin'."

"Looks like this time it's here to stay. Thank you momma'."

"Thank me for what?"

"For believing in me."

"You can thank yourself for that because I'm still not convince yet. There's one more task that awaits you outside those gates of yours and that's your home and where it's gonna' stand after you two finally meet face-to-face for the first time in over eighteen months."

"That shouldn't be too much of a problem. The divorce papers been sign. The house, she can have. Just give me my convertible, allow me to visit my kids until I get myself establish and the rest is history. I don't have no bad vibe towards her or anything. I come to realize one thing during my long stay away and that is what ever mistake made in life, one must first be willing to accept it as well as correct it. An apology might not make things better between us but at least it'll place my heart at a state of ease a lil'. That girl done nothing but love me the best way she knew how and that alone counts for a lot."

"And you just finding that out? HA! I knew you was a lil' slow but not THAT slow."

"Anyway, what's done is done and life goes on. So must I."

"You'll be aiight' son."

"Let me get off this phone momma' and don't forget to bring my kids with you when you pick me up tomorrow.'

"BOY, don't you think I got sense enough to know you would want me to bring my grandbabies with me? Son, we might be of the same lineage but definitely not of the same mentality."

"I love you too momma'."

"Bye young man. Love you too."

CHAPTER 66

"Red-Eyes, soljah bwoy, it's been fun but I gotta' run. One thing for certain, you'll be missed. I'm definitely gonna' keep in touch with you. You got my word on that."

"Bredren, me see meny cum an meny go but yu bredren, yu will be wun tu rememba. Me know yur man of ur wurd. One who speak frum de hart." He dug in his locker and pulled out a Rastah crown. "A gift bredren. Wear it wen yu feelen de leaf and not de need. Now go. Freetom waits yu."

Nard folded the crown and placed it in the book bag hanging from his shoulder.

"Give thanks bredren. I guess I'll be goen' now. Take care yourself celly."

He didn't know rather to hug or shake his hand and instead, pounded a fist over his heart twice.

"Bredren, dis no time tu go an get sof pon me. Get outta here! Yur runnen late."

The compound lacked any sight of inmates on his way to R&D (Receiving and Discharge). He wanted to consult with several of his associates one last time but work call over thirty minutes ago disallowed him the chance. A C.O. greeted him at the door with the clothes he had sent in from home to change out in. He studied his new look in the bathroom mirror. A perfect fit! "It's on pimpy'!" An identification card and check for $25's completed his remaining stay in R&D before being escorted to the institution front office. Ms. Cooper sat in the lobby. Smiling.

"You didn't think you was going to leave without saying goodbye to me first did you Mr. Hick?"

"I kind of figured you would pop-out from behind one of these doors."

"You mind if I escort you through the front door?"

"Please, by all means." She took hold of the door handle pulling it open for him to walk through first. "So this is what freedom feels like?"

"You like?"

"Do I like you ask? How bout' come ride with me and I'll show you just how much freedom REALLY means."

"Aren't we a lil' naughty. But unfortunately, my job awaits me."

"You be careful inside those gates sexy."

"I will. You be careful at home. And try being more careful with who you ride with the next time okay."

"Will do and that's for certain. Stacey?"

"Nard?" He searched for the right words to say but struggled. "I understand Mr. Hick. Now get out of here."

He searched the parking lot. A convertible Mercedes Benz exactly the same as his was parked a couple of rows off to his left. No one inside it. He walked on over. The tag on the back of it was exactly like his.

"Excuse me sir but…remember me?"

He froze in his stance. 'That voice! Could it have been? Impossible! Wouldn't hurt to try.' He turned around and couldn't believe what he saw.

"I'm sorry Nard. I hope you can find it somewhere in your heart to forgive me."

Her smile appeared brighter than he ever could imagine. He knelt down on one knee taking hold of her hand and looked up into her eyes.

"Mrs. Shontae Hick, would you mind loving me all over again?"

Eyes swelling with tears, "YES! Yes, I would love to Mr. Bernard Hick!"

PRESENT TIME

CHAPTER 67

"Oops, I almost forgot something," hurrying back to her gravesite. "One more thing I forgot to mention to you grandma'. Once my time is finally up on this God green earth of ours and I'm up there eaten' some of your delicious fried chicken with you again, just know one thing...nobody, and I mean NOBODY beats your chicken when it's Jarrett's delicious! I love you grandma' and have a nice day."

THE END...but we'll soon do it again!

Edwards Brothers Malloy
Ann Arbor MI. USA
May 10, 2017